MALLORY

OF THE

ANGELS

Conquest of Hell

CARLOS T. LEON

WestBow Press books may be ordered through booksellers or by contacting:

WestBow Press
A Division of Thomas Nelson & Zondervan
1663 Liberty Drive
Bloomington, IN 47403
www.westbowpress.com
1 (866) 928-1240

ISBN: 978-1-5127-3271-9 (sc)
ISBN: 978-1-5127-3272-6 (e)

Print information available on the last page.

WestBow Press rev. date: 02/26/2016

WESTBOW
P R E S S®
A DIVISION OF THOMAS NELSON
& ZONDERVAN

CHAPTER ONE - GOD'S ASSIGNMENT AND PROCLAMATION.

God Almighty, sitting in a heavenly cloud, requested the presence of all Archangels, Saints, **Jesus**, Angel Generals, and all important figures that had assisted God throughout time.

I God, have gathered you here so that "I" can explain my next mission. After **Jesus**, my Son, was Crucified, I asked **Jesus** to enter in to Hell. His mission was to assess Hell and to bring back as many Souls as he could.

Jesus explained to "**Me**" that there were many Souls who wanted to come back to the **Light of God,** but because of all the demon armies pushing them away from **Jesus**, many Souls could not be saved at that time. **Jesus** noted that the devils and demons waited just outside his range of light and attacked any Souls who wanted to approach **Jesus** to be saved. **Jesus** noted that if **He** had help to ward off the demos and devils, He could save most, if not all of the Souls wanting forgiveness. **Jesus** explained that in addition to the seven entrances to Hell, Lucifer had constructed three secret exits from Hell in which devils and demons could escape to Earth and not be discovered until these demons and devils had created havoc on Earth.

Based on **Jesus**' observations, **I, God**, have decided the following: As everyone in Heaven knows, Lucifer was once one of my prized Angels. He convinced many other Angels to follow him in an attempt to overthrow my Kingdom. Lucifer was expelled to Hell after his defeat by Michael the Archangel and the Armies of **God**.

Since **I, God**, gave humans the right to choose right from wrong, Lucifer has used this freedom of choice to corrupt as many Souls as possible. Lucifer has also tried to keep Souls from being in the Light of **God**.

I, God, have decided that Lucifer's actions must be stopped.

I God, have decided to offer Lucifer and his followers **permanent forgiveness** and bring each of them back into **Light of God**. Lucifer and his followers would have to pledge allegiance to God and the Rules of Heaven. Only those who Embrace the **Light of God** would be forgiven. All devils who do not accept the offer, will be Permanently destroyed. This offer includes Lucifer and any prior Angel of heaven who followed Lucifer's lead.

"God, in his glorious. Loving and Majestic Power, Summoning all the Heaven's forces together to Announce the War against Lucifer and all Evil."

"Jesus Describing his visit to hell and being surrounded by demons and devils who would not let him near souls that wanted to be saved."

"Lucifer as he appeared to Jesus, informing Jesus
that he was now in Hell, Lucifer's territory."

"**I God**", expect a very furious fight with Lucifer and his forces and many of **My** Angels will be hurt or seriously wounded, "**I God**" have declared that in this war in Hades, none of my Angels will suffer death. All wounded Angels will be Treated by the **Angels of Light** and be sent to Heaven to recuperate. Only Lucifer, devils, demons, and devil hounds will suffer permanent death of their Souls. Any mortally wounded devil or demon requesting forgiveness from **God** will be spared. **I God** want a specific military strategies from each of my Angel Generals, my Archangels, Jesus, and Mallory of the Angels. Archangel Michael will review all plans of attack and make any changes as needed. **I God**, will retain Michael the Archangel, the Apostles, Mother Mary, Jesus, and two Angel armies to remain in heaven with me to protect the gates of Heaven. "**I God**" have many strong and beautiful Angels to chose from to be "**My**" Special Envoy who will deliver my ultimatum to Lucifer. "**I God**" have chosen **Mallory of the Angels** to be the Angel that will go face to face with Lucifer and deliver to him my message of his forgiveness or his destruction.. I will select three of my warrior Archangels to stand by her side and protect her in her voyage and mission through Hades. **Mallory of the Angels** is an Angel of extreme Light and has the Light second only to that of Mother Mary. She also has courage and strength. She is pure, full of love and life. She is loved by all of the Angels in Heaven and has a Heavenly soft, tender touch . She is acknowledged to be the Angel Queen of Forgiveness. All Archangels hold her in high esteem. The three warrior Archangels that I have selected to protect Mallory of the Angels while she delivers my message are: **General Solrac, General Samot, and General Noel**. Many times these three Angels have been assigned to enter Hell on recon missions and have succeeded in each of their adventures in Perdition. Each of these Generals have proven their faithfulness to **Me, God**, by guarding the gates of Hell and defeating all the demon armies that attempted to escape Hell. I have all the confidence in them to protect **Mallory of the Angels.** "**I God,**" express "**My**" confidence in all "**My**" warriors, and their armies, who will at **My** command, enter Hell and either save all that want to be in "**My Light**, or destroy all demons who utterly refuse forgiveness. Any devil who lies about wanting forgiveness will be discovered, and will be burned without mercy, in **God's Light**.

"Mallory of the Angels listening to God's speech regarding the fight against all evil and the role she will play in God's Master Plan."

CHAPTER TWO - DESCRIPTION OF THE ANGEL ARMY TO FIGHT IN UNDERWORLD:

God's special envoy - Mallory of the Angels

Generals: (Total of **14 Generals**)

1. **Solrac** - Protect Mallory of the Angels and defeat Lucifer if needed.
2. **Samot** - Protect Mallory of the Angels and defeat Lucifer' body guards.
3. **Noel** - Protect Mallory of the Angels and assist Solrac and Samot.

For the Attack of Hell's exits:

4. **Esmeraldo L.**-assigned gate #1 Accompanied by Angel of Light Juana O.
5. **Richard O**. - Assigned exit gate # 2 accompanied by Angel of Light Margarit F.

6. **Juan aka Ponce** - Assigned Hell's gate #3 Accompanied by Angel of Light Digna Merida

For the attack of Hell's entrances:

7. **Augusto L.** -Hell's Entrance gate #1 Accompanied by Angel of Light Josefina. (Augusto will be God's Leading General)

8. **Eduardo E. aka Eddie** - Hell's entrance gate # 2 accompanied by Angel of Light Jaime

9. **Harry** - Hell's entrance gate #3 Accompanied by Angel of Light Juan-Jose.

10. **Petr O**. - Entrance Hell's gate # 4 Accompanied by Angel of Light and Love - Kris O.

11. **Esmeraldo B**. - Hell's gate # 5 Accompanied by Angel of Light **Santiago B**.

12. **Mr. Gabriel** - Hell's gate # 6 Accompanied by Angel of Light Sofia.

13. **John Richard M**. - Hell's gate # 7 accompanied by Angel of Light Saul

14. **Raymond** - Transportation -accompanied by Angel of Light Esperanza.

CHAPTER THREE - COMPOSITION OF THE ANGEL ARMIES;

Each of the Angel Armies will be filled by the following provisions:

1. One Angel General
2. 26 Archangels
3. 30,000 fighting Angels
4. 5,000 Healing Angels
5. 3,000 Angels of Light in addition to those accompanying the Generals
6. 2,000 Transportation Angels

All Angels will be involved in the battle except:

The Healing Angels who will heal any wounded Angel, as well any devil or lost Soul who wish to return to the Light of G**od**.

The Angels of Light will reform any devil or Soul who repents and wants to return to the Light of **God.**

The Transportation Angels are charged with transporting wounded Angels back to the safety of Heaven. They will also transport any devil or lost Soul who have converted back into the Light of **God**.

There will be one million Angels under the direct command of **Jesus** and Michael the Archangel. These Angels will stand ready to protect the Gates of Heaven in the event devils attempt an overt attack on the **Kingdom of Heaven**.

Approximately 5 million Angels will be involved in the great battle for the conquest of Hell, and once and for all, end Lucifer's reign. These Angels are sent with the mission of destroying all devils, demons, and demon hounds and destroying Hell's within its confines as needed.

CHAPTER FOUR - LOCATIONS OF ENTRANCES AND EXITS OF HELL:

The list below are the Modern and current locations to the entrances of the gates of Hell. All prior entrances were destroyed by the Devil or military leaders not wanting the gates of Hell in their location The Devil himself decided to make new entrances to Hell based on the locations that have lost or are losing the **Light of God.** Most evil people know of these entrances.

Entrances location:

1. Washington, D.C., U.S.A.
2. Havana, Cuba.
3. Medellin, Columbia, S.A.
4. Tijuana, Mexico.
5. Pyongang, North Korea.
6. Damascus, Syria.
7. Baghdad, Iraq

Because the new 7 entrances to Hell were known and guarded by the Forces of God, The Devil decided to create **3 secret exits** from Hell that He or his demons/devils could sneak out into the world and not be notice by the forces of God. Unfortunate for the Devil, **God** found out about these

Newly created exits and kept the findings a secret from Lucifer.

Exits location:

1. Mogadishu, Somalia
2. Hanoi, Viet-Nam
3. Juarez, Mexico.

CHAPTER FIVE - DESCRIPTION: INFERNO ONE

Modern Hell is divided into seven sections. Each section has it's own specific means of torture and punishment. Each section of Hell is divided by rivers of flowing lava which can only be crossed by high suspended metal bridges. Six metal bridges per section. Four bridges are for level transferring punished souls that need to be moved to a higher lever of torment. Two bridges are used for devils and demons who need to cross to another section. Souls that are being transferred have to walk on a hot metal bridge, heated by the hot lava to a minimum of 1200 degrees F. The brides are greased and slippery and sway violently. They are meant to cause falls and slips. The two bridges used by the devils/demons are smooth and not heated or treated with razors, glass, or nails.

Inferno 1 is the first stop for all wayward Souls. At this stop, each Soul is evaluated for levels of punishment and torture. The first things the Souls see are **hideous demons** of all shapes and sizes. Ugly is a mild word to describe their facial features. The eyes are not symmetrical and of various colors, mainly red or yellow. They have pus sores throughout their faces. Their noses are beak like or dog like, with foul smelling mucus that never stop flowing out of their noses. The ears are bat-like, some with cartilage, some without giving them a floppy ear appearance. The mouth is fowl smelling with rotten gums, rotten tongues, and teeth like spikes and nails with three inch fang-like teeth that hang over the bottom lip when their mouth is closed. They have a roar that deadens your eardrums and cause pain in your temples, eyes, and head. Their arms are triple the size of human arms with claws like bears or komodo dragons.

These demons take pride in frightening their captors and with continuing cruelty, hurting them often.

The bodies differ in so many ways that you could be looking at a giant human lizard, a lion/hyena mix, hound like with large hind legs and small front legs. The shoulders have lumps of decaying meat that never seems to fall off. Each one has a large rat like tail that seem absent of hair or fur, except at the tip.

"Souls crossing the bridge from one Hell level to another level of Hell for further punishment."

CHAPTER SIX - INFERNO ONE - CONTINUED

These demon-like creatures continuously attack and harass you while other devils push the weary Souls in line to be evaluated. The devils are highly wicket and have no mercy what so ever. These devils too, come in various sizes. Most of them in **Inferno one** are green with red faces. These have almost human like bodies except for their faces, head, hands, and feet.

The devils of **Inferno One** come in various shades of green with the one who leads or having the most power can be distinguished with a dark green. The shape of his head is almost human but it is slightly oblong with goat like horns on top. The head is supported by a skinny leather like neck. Their eyes are glowing red and are shaped like eggs. Their nose have just two button size holes that lay flat on their faces. The teeth are jagged, highly sharp and pointed. There is no space between the jagged teeth, The bottom row of teeth has a 2 inch fang on each side of the mouth. The main body resembles a human being except in size they tend to be 7 feet or taller. The hands tend to be long reaching their knees. The fingers are also long about 10 to 15 inches with razor sharp finger nails. They walk upright and can run faster than a normal dog.

Inferno one is mainly dark, the glow from the hot lava gives off a light like our sunset. The lava flows keep a steady stream of shimmering lights on the ceilings, walls, and floors. These shimmering lights add to the danger and increases the fear felt by the tortured Souls. **Inferno one** has fire poles spaced throughout the area to give minimum light so the Souls could see each other's suffering.

The smell in **Inferno One** is horrendous. It smells like brim-stone mixed with Smelling salt. The odor brings tears to their eyes, burns their nose, burns their throat and lungs, and adds to the horror of these Souls.. It is almost impossible to breath. The taste in your mouth and tongue makes you feel like wrenching or vomiting frequently.

All Souls enter **Inferno one** with the same body and capacity that they had in the living world. Each Soul enters **Inferno one** with a semi-bright yellow glow. This glow makes for easy recognition and marks the Souls for torture.

All Souls at each level, after torture or punishment, are restored fully to body and capacity, the next day so that torture and punishment can start all over again. Souls do not die Except if destroyed by GOD and his forces.

Chapter Seven - Inferno one - continued

The floors of **Inferno One are** extremely narrow and are meant to have Souls slip, slide or fall. The walking paths are greasy. On either side of the paths, there are broken glass, nails, razor blades, and jagged rocks. If a Souls does not slip or fall, the demons will push them off the path into harms way.

ALL SEVEN ENTRANCES TO HELL GO THROUG AND END UP IN IFERNO ONE

Inferno one is where each Soul is classified by the types of sins committed, and to which level of hell they will be transferred to for torture and punishment.

Classification of which level of Hell each Soul is to be assigned is handle in **Inferno one**. Souls are classified by the level of sins committed.

The classification process is meant to be as much punishment as possible so that the Souls get their first taste of Hell. While in line waiting for classification, the Souls are scratched, bitten, hit with clubs. Each devil is given specific Souls to torment, torture, and harass in what ever way will cause the most shock and pain. When the lead devil classifies a Soul, **Souls are then branded on their buttocks** with their level of Hell assigned to them.

Classification 1 is for **Inferno one**. (**previously described** in start of chapter 4)

This level is for assessment of sins committed and level of classification.

Classification 2 is for **Inferno two**.

This level is for bullies, adulterers, thieves, those that commit manslaughter, and frequent crime offenders.

Classification 3 if for **Inferno three**.

This level is for those who sinned against life, such as purposely injuring people or animals. killing or injuring disabled persons. Internet thieves and ID theft.

Classification 4 is for **Inferno four**.

This level is for rapists, drunk driver killers; those that committed sex crimes against the innocent.

Classification 5 is for **Inferno five**.

This level is for suicides, those who have purposely taken the life of a child or infants

Classification 6 is for **Inferno six**.

This level is for murderers, atheists, Hollywood actors who support communism, and crimes against God and the Church.

Classification 7 is for **Inferno seven**.

This level is the Devil's playground in which Lucifer maintains his personal mansion. Souls that did not receive a classification from **Inferno one,** or who committed very unusual sins, are sent to this level. In addition, Lucifer also summons Souls from each Hell level to entertain his elite group of devils.

Inferno seven is also the level where the **three new exits** from Hell are located. These exits were built in secrecy to prevent the forces of Heaven from knowing about them. Lucifer and his devils believed that all of God's forces would be guarding only the other entrances to Hell. (**Not so!)**

Level seven is also where Lucifer **trains his devils** for special assignment on earth.

CHAPTER EIGHT - INFERNO TWO. LOCATED ONE LEVEL BELOW INFERNO ONE

Hell two is the **level of fire**. and it is connected to **Inferno one** by six bridges, four bridges for transferring Souls, and two for the devils and demons to move from level to level.

Inferno two has the most lava flow and the worst smell of brimstone and decay. The devils have gruesome features, their heads are a mix of a Komodo dragon and alligator. The mouth is oblong but the snout pushes way forward like an alligator. The tongue has a three way split like a pitchfork. The teeth are razor sharp with each tooth measuring seven inches long and the fangs measuring as much as one foot in length. Their breath is fowl smelling and they can spit a flame of fire that can reach up to 40 feet in the air and spread 15 feet wide.

These devils are built for flight and have powerful, tough, leathery wings. When they start to fly, Souls caught underneath their powerful wingspan will be pushed back 20 feet.

The devils in **Inferno three** have large bodies, large heads, and the feet resemble those of the T-Rex dinosaur. Their five feet long arms are located on shoulders that allow for 360 degrees rotation. Their long fingernails and claws are tough and made to cut concrete and steel to shred. These devils enjoy the heat, love the fire, and enjoy torturing the Souls in their area. These devils enjoy using their feet and teeth to scare and torture the Souls assigned to they level.

The demons enjoy handing out the harshest punishment to the **bullies**

Each Soul in Hell feels the pain as if they were alive in the living world.

Bullies would feel 40 times the punishment they gave to other. Afterwards, the smaller demons beat the bullies with fire torches. The torture continues all day and night and the next day the Souls get rejuvenated and the torture starts all over.

The adulterer, the thieves, those who have committed manslaughters, and the frequent crime offenders are taken to the lakes of lava and pushed in and allow to burn slowly. Since humans believed they would burn in Hell, the devils accommodated them to that experience. The devils push one Soul in at a time so that the Souls waiting to be pushed into the lava can see what is in store for them. The devils alternate who gets to be pushed in first and who goes in last. The last Soul to go in the hot lava were given additional pain and punishment. The smell of burning meat is prevalent in **Inferno two**.

The demon hounds in this level resemble pit-bulls, but their sizes are 5 times larger than any known pit-bull. The neck muscles have a circumference of 2 feet. Their claws are 4 inches long and sharp as a razor. The teeth will leave puncture holes of 2 inches deep. Their mouth measure 2 foot long. Their tails have spikes of steel which they use to snap and strike Souls. These hounds are merciless and are on attack mode every second of the day.

CHAPTER TEN - INFERNO THREE. - LOCATED ONE LEVEL BELOW INFERNO TWO

This level of **Hell** is known for the fun devils have in dishing out the pain and agony to the Souls assigned to them. The various types of pain causing machines they have in their disposal is unending. The devils in Inferno three love to record the sounds of torture emitted from the punished Souls and later play the sounds back to Souls awaiting their turn for torture. screams and groans of the Souls as they are being tortured. The next day the Souls are returned to normal either at the end of the punishment or at the beginning of the next day so they can relive the relentless gruesome torture.

The devils here love to place the **bullies** in first in the torture line.

Those who commit **crimes by cyber net or by identify theft** are first hanged by their thumbs and index finger for hours before being placed in the burning lava.

The devils in this level are between 3 to 4 feet tall and 5 feet wide. The devils have eight arms that are 6 feet long with fingers 18 inches long.

The fingernails are sharp and thick, meant for shredding skin. They have 2 heads, one on each side of the top of the body. Their eyes are bulging and are yellow-green in color. Their eyes are always glowing. They have four feet that are flat with pointy toes. Each head has a mouth full of rotten decaying sharp teeth also made for shredding and spreading germs to the Souls. The demon hounds in this level are shaped like scorpion fish with additional poison spikes surrounding their bodies. These hounds jump on the souls, knock them down the rolling over the Souls so that the spikes can cut and shred their skins. The wounds are allowed to go untreated. Both devils and hounds are a pasty white color.

CHAPTER ELEVEN - INFERNO FOUR:

The devils in this level are truly the experts in torturing Souls. The instruments or tools they prefer are meant to bring outright pain and suffering, the likes of which have never been know to mankind. The brutality of the punishment is too graphic to even put in print. In Inferno Four the greatest punishments were reserved for **Rapist and Sex offenders,**

Drunk drivers who kill or maim innocent people are given punishment to exact 40 times the pain or suffering they caused while on Earth. Many times the drunk drives where also marched to the burning lava and pushed in. For additional punishment, the drunk drivers where thrown into a snake pits that contained rattlers, cobra, Black mambas, and coral snakes.

The devils in Inferno four are fierce fighters and are feared by most other devils in Hell. They have almost human like features except that their heads have spikes throughout the head, including the face. The teeth resemble shark teeth. Their eyes glow Technicolor and never look the same. The body is like a 12 foot Grey back gorillas with arms that can tear man or beast in half. Their legs and feet are made for stomping as well as for running. These devils like to borrow and use the demon hounds from level two to attack the Souls while they are waiting for their punishment.

CHAPTER TWELVE -INFERNO FIVE. - LOCATED ONE LEVEL BELOW INFERNO FOUR

In this level, you will find the Souls of those who committed suicides, killers who have taken the lives of children or infants and those who started wild fires that caused injury or death to people and animals or in which homes or property are severely damaged or destroyed.

The devils in this level like to use old fashion torture. Souls in this level are tortured by stretching at the rack, burning their fingers, hanging upside down, and burning at the haystack. Since burning Souls is a known method of torture in Hades, the devil's favorite pass time was Burning Souls in the fire pits. Other inspiring torture was left up to the whim of the supervising devil.

When this is done, demon hounds that look like a giant six foot long dog with an alligator head, are let lose to run amuck among these Souls chopping and biting at will.

The devils in this level all have heads like Medusa, the snakes are real and bite Souls when the devils approaches them. Their eyes glow bright yellow and never blink. Their mouths is shaped like barracudas and have plenty of sharp teeth. Their bodies are greasy and have scales like fish. The trunk of their bodies are like a Beluga whale with crusty arms and legs. The arms have a giant lobster claw where the hands would be. The feet are one foot long and the toe nails are as hard as Brazil nuts.

The demon hounds are shaped like Montana Wolfs, with their bodies resembling a human hunchback. Their size are triple the size of a normal Wolf. Their heads are unsymmetrical with lumps throughout the head. They generally stand on all four legs, but at various times, they stand on two legs to attack. Their mouths resemble the Northern Pike fish, but quadrupled in size, with corresponding giant teeth. They have one foot long paws with ten toes each foot and each toe having 3 inch claws for scratching their victims. On four feet these hounds stand 6 feet tall.

CHAPTER THIRTEEN - INFERNO SIX. (LOCATED ONE LEVEL BELOW INFERNO FIVE.)

This level of Hell is primary for Murderers, Atheist, Hollywood actors that secretly supported communism while taking advantage of all America had to give them; and for persons who committed crimes against **God** and betraying the Church. (Betraying the Church means betraying the goodwill and the integrity of all religions, and all faiths, who in their own way, honor **God.**

The devils here are next in line to be moved up to Inferno seven. They are being prepared by Lucifer to advance in the art of deviltry.

The demon hounds glow red and have the bodies of gargoyles. They stand 8 foot tall and have various ferocious faces and teeth, They can fly and their legs are made for snatching Souls on the ground and flying them to any number of lava pits or torture chambers. Their arms are five feet long with hands containing 10 inch fingers with sharp claws that are one inch thick and four inches long. These demon hounds are permitted to attack any Soul they want and punish them as long as they want. These hounds keep the Souls in line so that the devils can instill the punishment due them.

The devils here can be described as 12 feet tall, grayish in color, with elongated scaly face that resemble a dragon. The head is 2 feet in diameter and is covered with boils and pustules. In fact, you can find boils and pustules all over the body. The eyes are 3 inches round and they flicker like flames of fire red, green and yellow. The mouth extends four inches from the face with razor sharp teeth. On the bottom set of teeth they have two 4 inch eye teeth. The spine has multiple sharp spines that go from tail to the top of the back of the head. The top of the head has four horns that resemble the horns on the cartoon Maleficent with black and gold stripes. The tail just manage to touch the ground with eight one foot sharp metal spikes. The shoulders and arms are muscle bound and the hands and fingers are made for grabbing and tearing flesh. The legs are very powerful and their feet can crush and flatten steel balls the size of basketballs. These tricky devils can shift-change.

CHAPTER FOURTEEN - INFERNO SIX - CONTINUED.

The tools of these devils at this level are very simple but effective. For murderers and Atheists the devils attack them with rusty pitchforks. The devils have many ways to use the pitchforks and they enjoy using each method of pitchfork torture on each Soul in their section. Afterwards, the Souls are taken to the dog pit where the Souls are turned lose to run for their lives as demon hounds chase after them to bite and scratch. After the dog pit, the torn Souls are placed in a fire tunnel and made to run barefoot through the fire. The Souls are then restored and the punishment starts all over again.

For Hollywood actors that secretly support communism while taking advantage of all of America's goodness and income, these Souls are given the same punishment as the Atheists and are also given additional punishment such as cleaning up the toilets, cleaning the mock off the floors, and bathing the devils until they are squeaky clean. Then afterwards, they are placed in poison ivy and poison sumac plants without treatment. When this is done, the devils escort these souls to the lava pits where each is branded with a cattle iron, a "star", and pushed into the lava pit. The Souls that committed crime against God and the Church were given the same punishment as the murderers and in addition, where placed in burning oil

The Souls in Inferno six do no rest. As soon as they finish a punishment, they are restored immediately so they could suffer each torture to the fullest.

Chapter Fifteen - Inferno seven: (one level below Inferno six and the last level of Hell)

This level of Hell contains no demon hounds nor other devils that have not been personally invited by Lucifer. Any demon hound or devil that accidentally enters level seven without permission, are subject for torture at Lucifer's will.

The devils in this level are completely different from the devils located in any of the six Inferno of Hell. These devils have complete human features and lived and had experience human life on Earth. Each of these devils are as different in size, shape, and form, as there are different human beings.

These devils have been especially selected by Lucifer from the other levels of Hell. Lucifer especially like to pick devils who were like leeches, who while on their mission on earth, sucked out the life and goodness of humans. As a gift for their ferocity and eagerness to torture Souls, Lucifer transformed them from their gross monstrous form to human like appearance. Each male and female devil became very good looking, but because Lucifer is the only one that is perfect in Hell, these devils all would have a slight scar on their forehead and on their chest or upper back. This Lucifer call the "**devil's mark**". Each devil in Inferno seven is given a charming personality to be able to charm the human beings they are assigned to corrupt. The exception to the selection process for devils in **Inferno seven** include the 100 **fallen angels** who followed Lucifer to Hell. These fallen Angels automatically live and work in Lucifer's Mansion. Here, at this level, Lucifer trains these selected devils for their special assignment, i.e., each devil is expected to create confusion and havoc on Earth. Souls who have committed horrendous crimes or murder on Earth, are given a chance to pledge their loyalty to Lucifer after spending one month of punishment at their selected level of Hell. The devils in Inferno seven leave and return via the three secret exits. While waiting for their assignments, these devils are treated to special torture events to wet their appetite for torture. These special events are held in **Lucifer's Mansion**. Lucifer's describes his mansion "as his heaven in Hell", His official play ground. All of Lucifer's wishes come true for him in his mansion. The mansion is as long as two football fields and surrounded by a moat that contains flowing hot lava. The mansion is square in shape and holds a court yard in the center the size of a football field. The entrance doors are platted in gold.

The bottom rooms of the five stories open to this courtyard. The mansion contains 3000 rooms for sleeping or resting when the devils are not at work.

These rooms have all the comfort of a five star hotel. Some Souls that have dedicated their service to Lucifer, but who were not hand picked for level seven, are used as maids, ushers or chefs.

There are 24 swimming pools, each the size of an Olympic pool. There are 40 rooms that are use to parade naked Souls, for selection of sex with devils in Inferno seven. The sex administered here is not a meant for pleasure, but to be extremely painful to the Souls.

The center court is used for mass meetings, for celebrations, and at certain times, Souls are let loose in the court to be chased and capture by the devils for torture and punishment.

There are 100 torture rooms, the size of a basketball court, with a seating capacity of 200. These rooms contain all the torture equipment found in the other levels of hell. Lucifer has placed the 100 fallen Angels that followed him to Hell in charge of these torture rooms.

There is one room that is 600 feet square and has a special torture device that is only used by Lucifer himself. This room has a seating capacity of 1000 seats. In this room there is a razor blade 50 foot long, extremely sharp and firm enough to hold a Soul that weighs up to 700 pounds.

This mansion was completed as a rewards for Lucifer and his selected, trusted devils. **Lucifer has two body guards, the Soul of a super atheist, who he calls Moe, for her initials of M.O. His other body guard is the Soul of Hitler.** Lucifer has taught his body guards to be ruthless, dangerous, intelligent, and completely loyal to Him.

Lucifer selects a variety of Souls from each level of Perdition to be tortured by his selected devils in Inferno seven. In addition, any Soul that could not be classified in **level one** or who committed extraordinary sins, are sent to level seven for punishment.

Looking at his domain, Lucifer is satisfied. Each Inferno level is 50 square miles each and the areas are composed of dry melted lava, mountains of jagged rocks, and in semi-darkness except for the lava flow and the glow of the fire poles. His mansion is also well lighted.

CHAPTER SEVENTEEN - INFERNO SEVEN - CONTINUED:

With the exception of **Inferno seven**, each level of Hell smells like sulfa and brimstone. Breathing is almost impossible. The floors contain decaying pieces of meat, vomit, feces, urine, slime, sweat, grease and blood. If a person could envision Earth at its beginning, the heat and melting lava would be just like the Hell of today.

The Souls are always slipping, sliding, falling, or pushed to the floor. The howls and yells of pain and distress are never ending. The floors all contain broken pieces of glass, sharp nails, razors, and jagged rocks. The heat from the lava flow is horrendous causing Souls to lose fluid and become dehydrated immediately. There are no breezes nor open doors for circulation. The floor bubbles with underlying lava flow and are painfully hot to walk on. Smoke is everywhere and causing the eyes of the Souls to water and unable to see properly. Each level of Lucifer's Inferno is directly under the other forming 7 levels with 6 connecting bridges. The bridges are guarded by four demons each. Modern Hell resembles a very large stairway to move Souls up or down as needed. In total, **Lucifer has 8 million devils under his command.** They torture and punish Souls sent to Hell by **God** and his Forces. The **Souls in Hell number in the tenth of million**. The **fallen angels** that followed Lucifer to Hell start their day by selecting the Souls to be tortured and selecting the tools and means of torture to be used in their torture room. These fallen angels have up to 100 human like devils to assist them with the torturing. The Souls are kept for 24 hours in any one torture room, and after the Souls are restored, they are transferred to another fallen angel's chamber to suffer another brand of torture.

Because of the selections of special devils to **Inferno seven**, Lucifer knows that the pain inflicted here will be at minimum, three times worse than at any other level of Hell. Being picked for **Inferno seven** is an improvement in devil status and each of these devils take pride in the benefits granted them. Torture is the name of the game and the randomly selected Souls are in for a nightmare of torture and pain.

Although the selection to Lucifer's torture room is by randomly selecting the worse Soul of each level, Lucifer enjoys selecting the crimes against God, murderers, and those that kill children and infants. These He reserves for his 50 foot long razor slide.

CHAPTER EIGHTEEN - INFERNO SEVEN - CONTINUED

Lucifer's torture room has a giant razor blade, very sharp, and greased from top to bottom. The razor blade stands 50 feet at the top and is angled downward so that the end of the razor is just one foot above the ground. The razor itself has a 7 foot shaft underneath to support the sharp end of the blade. The Souls, before being sat on the razor, have their bottoms greased to overflowing. Because the razor blade torture is the worst type of torture in Hell, Lucifer reserves this method of torture for the truly wicked sinner.

Lucifer has a varied reservoir of devils to select for assignments on Earth.

Here at this level, Lucifer trains each devil for the assignment given him/her. Lucifer likes to target Ministers, Priests, Deacons of the Church, all high ranking church positions, men and women of political power, men and women in control of business, and just about any ordinary human in the **Grace of God** that the devils can easily corrupt. These trained devils leave and return to **Inferno seven** of Hades by the 3 secret exits that Lucifer created for this purpose. As Lucifer believed these exits "secret" and not known to the forces of God, He placed a minimum detachment of 10 devils to maintain guard at each gate. When devils in Level seven fight, they revert from their human form to their fierce devil or demon form**.**

CHAPTER NINETEEN - PLANNING THE ATTACK ON HELL AND EARTH.

After consulting with **Jesus**, Archangels, Generals, Saints, Apostles, Mother Mary, Earth Angels, Angels of Light, and Mallory of the Angels, **I, God,** have approved the attack plan to start promptly at 6 p.m. on July 10th.

All of the Earth Angels, listed below with their individual heavenly rank, will be given Angel Status, along with Angel wings, for as long as the fight to conquer Hell is completed. These Earth Angels will be given the Honor of striking the first blow of the war. When the war is over, these Earth Angles will return to their normal lives as Humans.

Archangels on Earth:

Nancy B., Maria R., Inez M., Esperanza L., Nelly R., Camille H., Gloria L., Lucy A., Monica N., Bridget D., Juanita S., Juanita (Jenny) M., Aladin K., Catherine L., Cathy T., Sarah L., Ashley L., Vicki C., Andrew M., David S., Paul H.G. (**Camille H. will be the Archangel in Charge)**

Angel Generals on Earth:

Carlos II, Richard L, Carlos III, Big D, Jaqueline, Ono, Tomas N., Jesse D., Joey CSM, Johnny M., John M., John T., Marius N., Rene D.T., Esteban B., Jose B., Carlos B., Junior, Johnny D., George L., Bert M., Teo M.,

Chuck K., Roger R., Terry S., Bill M., Zack., Eddie R., Chuck R., Ric O.,

Ken & Olga U., Cynthia M, Richard W., Eddie R., Johannes Maximus

Alexus and Matthew.

(Carlos II will be the Angel General in Charge.)

Angels of Light & Love on Earth:

Christina S., Lois, Lilly G., Joyce N., Don R., Alana, Nympha M., Jade M.,

Penny R., Judy S., Sandy M., Carry M., Heather O., Janet, Lara M.,

Andrea O., Teresa A., Caleb R. Carter R., (AKA the Bomb ones Brothers), Amy H., Cheffy R., Chana R., Chickie R., Jacqueline, Jennifer, George. (**Caleb R and Carter R will be the Angels of light and love in Charge.**

In addition to the Earth Angels of Light and Love assigned to the Earth Archangels and the Earth Angel Generals, Heaven will provide an additional 15,000 fighting Angels and 3,000 Transportation Angels to each.

The assignment for the battle on Earth will take place by dividing the Earth into seven sections, representing **the seven continents of Earth**. North America, South America, Europe, Africa, Asia, Australia and Antarctica.

Chapter Twenty - Planning the attack on Hell and Earth: Continued

North America: Will have the following Earth Angels assigned:
Archangels; Nancy B., Maria R., Inez M., and Esperanza L., Camille H.
Angel Generals: Carlos II, Richard L., Carlos III, Big D. Ono, Cynthia M., Mathew.
Angels of Light: Christina S., Lois K., Lilly G., Joyce N.
Supporting Angels: 252,000.00
NOTE: (Camille H. will be the Archangel in charge of Earth Angels)
(Carlos L. II will be the General in charge of Earth Angels)

(Caleb and Carter R. will be Light Angels in Charge on Earth)

South America: Will have the following Earth Angels assigned:

Archangels: Nelly R. Gloria L., Lucy A., and Monica N.

Angel Generals: Jesse D., Joey R. CSM, Johnny M., John T., Marius N., Rene D.T.,

Angels of Light: Don R, Alana, Nympha M., Jade M., Jacqueline,

Supporting Angels: 270,000.00

Europe: Will have the following Earth Angels assigned:

Archangels: Bridget D., Juanita S., Juanita/Jenny M., Aladin K.

Angel Generals: Esteban B., Jose B., Carlos B., Junior E., Johnny D., George L., Bert M., George

Angel of Light: Penny R., Judy S., Sandy M., Carey G., Jenifer.

Supporting Angels: 270,000.00

Africa: Will have the following Earth Angels assigned:

Archangels: Catherine L., Cathy T., Sarah L, Ashley L,

Angel Generals: Teo M., Chuck K., Roger R., Terry S., Bill M,. Zack.

Angels of Light: Heather O., Janet, Lara M.

Supporting Angels: 234,000.00

CHAPTER TWENTY ONE - PLANNING THE ATTACK ON HELL AND EARTH - CONT. ASIA: WILL HAVE THE FOLLOWING EARTH ANGELS ASSIGNED:

Archangels: Richard & Susanna W., Andrew M., Paul H.G.

Angel Generals: Eddie R., Chucky R., Ric O., Ken & Olga U.

Angels of Light: Caleb R. and Carter R. (aka: Inez's Bombones) Andrea O., Teresa A.

Supporting Angels: 280,000.00

Australia: Will have the following Earth Angels assigned:

Archangels: Alexis, Vicki C. & Larry J.

Angel General: Amy H., Arty M.

Angels of Light: Joann R., Sylvia R.

Supporting Angels: 90,000.00

Antarctica: Will have the following Earth Angels assigned:

Archangels: David S.

Angel Generals: Kevin N., Scott N.

Angel of Light: Maria A.

Supporting Angels: 54,000.00

Throughout the fight on earth, all Armies needing help will request help from Angel General Carlos II, who will distribute assets as needed. If more help is needed, Michael the Archangel will send additional help from the Angel Armies protecting the Gates to Heaven. In addition, as new Earth Angels are recognized, these Earth Angels will be added to the Earth Armies.

Once all the Earth Angels are given Angel Status by **God**, these Earth Angels will automatically receive the power and knowledge of all Angels and will receive instant communications from God and Archangels.

CHAPTER TWENTY TWO - LET THE FIGHT ON EARTH BEGIN:

A vital part of **God's** attack on evil forces on Earth is the use of **Greenwich Mean time (GMT)**. Greenwich Mean Time is a method that divides the Earth into 24 separate time zones. By using GMT, the attack will start precisely at 6 pm, regardless of where on earth you find yourself in. The attack, timed and coordinated precisely at 6 pm, will cause great confusion and disrupt Lucifer's forces on Earth the ability to mount a counter-attack.

On July 10th at 6:00 p.m., GMT, as the order to attack was being sounded, **God** sent out a brilliant, continuous, flash of light that illuminated all Souls, demons, devils, hell hounds, and evil Souls on Earth. The brilliance of these light rays were a trillion times brighter than the Star of Bethlehem, each ray resembling a magnificent, giant, glowing cross in the sky. A brilliant cross of light that brought the love and warmth of **God** to Earth. This glow from heaven made it so that there was no place on Earth where evil could hide or that **God's** light did not reach.

God also gave His light the ability to give all evil forces a permanent red glow, and to stop for two full minutes, all movement, all activities, and all communications between all red glowing individual on Earth. These two minutes were given to allow the Earth forces to locate and identify evil in their continent of assignment and bring the war to them. Any devil, demon, or hell hound attempting to leave Hell during this time would be disintegrated immediately.

If a person believed in **God**, no matter what religion he or she chose to worship, when touched by **God's** light, their Souls would emit a heavenly blue glow. These Souls would immediate feel the Love and Protection of **God** and were allowed to continue with their lives undisturbed by evil. The blue glow would remain until the battle for Earth was completed. These demons, devil, demon hound or a person who did not believe in **God**, such as an Atheist; or was an evil person who committed crimes against humanity or **God**, those who killed or committed crimes in the name of **God**, their Souls, when touched by Light sent by **God**, would give off a bright red glow, to remain red until the battle for Earth was over.

God deliberately made the evil forces on Earth glow red for quick identification and destruction or to give them the benevolent opportunity to repent and enter the Kingdom and the Light and Love of God.

CHAPTER TWENTY THREE - LET THE FIGHT ON EARTH BEGIN - CONTINUED.

God also commanded that once the battle for Earth began, under no circumstances, will any devil or demon be allowed to return to Hell. Any demon or devil trying to return to Hell will be destroyed immediately. All Souls glowing red, before being destroyed, will be given an opportunity to take the oath and pledge allegiance to God and Heaven. Any devil or demon giving a false or insincere request asking for God's forgiveness will immediately be set aside and their Soul destroyed. Devils and demons who seem to have a sincere request for forgiveness will be transported to Hell one where a camp has been set aside for further evaluation of their sincerity. If the oath is sincerely and truthful, these Souls will be transported to heaven and receive the Forgiveness and Love of **God**.

In His most Holiest Wisdom, God realized that the fight on Earth would not take longer than a few months, but in those few months, many of his Earth Angels would suffer many casualties, but as He declared, no Angel will die.

God knew in his heart that the real fight, the toughest fight, would be waiting for his warriors who would enter the gates and the fires of Hell. These Heavenly warriors will be facing Lucifer and his toughest and meanest evil army in the Underworld.

Not like in Earth, where the evil forces were illuminated in red, the devils in Hell could look like the Angels themselves, and present a greater danger in fighting them. **God** believes that many devils and Souls serving time in Hell will want to convert to His love and therefore, weaken the forces of Hell.

Chapter Twenty four - Let the fight on Earth begin - North America

At 6 p.m. GMT, and after 2 minutes **God**'s light was seen to illuminated all evil figures red, General Carlos II and Archangel Camille H. sounded the alarm to begin the attack on Earth. Immediately, the forces of Earth Angels Struck fear and death in their continent area of assignment.

In North America, the immediate and severe problem areas facing the Earth Angels were Juarez, Mexico, Tijuana, Mexico, Washington D.C., Chicago, Illinois, Detroit Michigan, New York City, New York, Los Angeles, California, Sacramento, California, and Havana, Cuba. The other areas in North America were giving mild to moderate problems.

"Lucifer, as He has his eyes on his prized possession, the Earth."

North America - continued.

General Carlos II attacked the red glowing evil in Juarez, Mexico.

Archangel Camille H. attack the red glowing figures in Tijuana, Mexico.

General Richard L. attacked the red glowing figures in Washington, D.C.

Archangel Nancy B. attacked the red glowing figures in Chicago, Ill.

General Carlos L. III attacked the red glowing figures in Detroit, Mich.

Archangel Maria R. attacked the red glowing figures in NYC, New York.

General Darion (aka Big D) attacked the red figures in L.A., Calif.

Archangel Inez M. attacked the red glowing figures in Havana, Cuba.

General Ono attacked the red glowing figures in Sacramento, Calif.

General Cynthia M., and Archangel Esperanza L. attacked all other areas in North America and the Caribbean Island not covered by other forces.

Each General and Archangel attacked their area supported by 10,000 fighting Angels. The exception being that General Cynthia M. and Archangel Esperanza L., with 152, 000 fighting Angels, attacked the remaining areas of North America and the Caribbean while providing support to the other fighting forces in North America as needed.

The plan in North America succeeded as **God** commanded. In ten weeks, all figures glowing red were cornered and engaged in severe combat. Over 30,000 Angels were wounded in the combat. These wounded Angels were immediately transported to Heaven for healing and the protection of **God** and His heavenly forces.

17 million devils, demons, demon hounds, and evil Souls were completely destroyed in heavy hand to hand combat.

The Angels of Light and Love, Christina S., Lois K., Lilly G., and Joyce N., were able to save 33 million Souls and devils who repented and pledge their allegiance to **God** and Heaven.

The entire campaign in North America lasted only 10 weeks. **Angel General Carlos II, Gen. Big D,** and **Archangel Camille H.** proclaimed to **God** that North America now rests in the arms of **God** and is now part of Heaven,.

CHAPTER TWENTY FIVE - LET THE FIGHT ON EARTH BEGIN - SOUTH AMERICA

In South America, the most pressing areas of evil strangulations are Rio de Genero, Brazil, Bogotá, Columbia, Medellin, Columbia, Georgetown, Guyana, Buenos Aires, Argentina, the Falkland, Island, Cayenne, French Guiana, and Caracas, Venezuela.

Within the 2 minutes of **God's** light shinning in South America, Archangel Nelly R., and Angel General Jesse D,. identified all the red glowing individuals and gave the order to begin the attack.

Archangel Nelly R, with 10,000 fighting Angels attacked Rio de Genero.

Angel General Jesse D. with 10,000 fighting Angels attacked Medellin,

Archangel Gloria L, with 10,000 fighting Angels attacked Caracas.

Angel General Joey R-CSM, with 10,000 fighting Angels attacked Bogotá.

Archangel Lucy A., with 10,000 fighting Angels attacked Buenos Aires.

Angel General Juan M., with 10,000 fighting Angels attacked Georgetown.

Archangel Juanita S, with 10,000 fighting Angels attacked the Falkland, Is

Angel General John T., with 10,000 Native Angels attacked Cayenne.

Angel Generals Marious N., and Rene D.T., with the balance of 190,000 fighting Angels attacked the rest of South America while providing assistance to any forces in South America needing Help.

The fight in South American lasted 9 weeks and cost 43,000 Angel Casualties. These wounded warriors where immediately transported to Heaven for medical treatment, rest, under the protection and love of **God**.

19 Million devils, demons, demon hounds, and evil Souls were completely destroyed without any mercy.

The Angels of Light and Love Don R., Alana, Nympha M., and Jade M., were able to save 52 million devils and Souls, and bring them to the light and love of **God**.

The battle campaign in South America lasted 15 weeks, all of which was non stop fighting and destruction.

At the end of the fighting, Angel Gen. **Jesse D**. and **Archangel Juanita S.** proclaimed to **God** that All of South American was in His hands and that South America was now a part of Heaven.

CHAPTER TWENTY SIX - LET THE FIGHT ON EARTH BEGIN - EUROPE

On July 10th, at 6 pm GMT, the forces assigned to Europe were ready for the signal to attack. As soon as **God** sent forth his brilliant light that paralyzed and made the evil forces in Europe glow red, Archangel Bridget D., and Angel General Esteban B., issued the signal to begin the attack.

The Earth force in Europe knew in advance that the strongest opposition would come from the following cities in Europe. Dublin, Ireland. Zaragoza, Spain. Palermo, Sicily. Moscow, Russia. Kiev, Russia. Belgrade, Serbia. Athens, Greece. Bagdad, Iraq. Damascus, Syria. Therefore, the assignments went as follows:

Archangel Bridget D., with 10,000 fighting angels attacked Bagdad.

Angel General Esteban B., with 10,000 fighting Angels attacked Damascus.

Archangel Monica N., with 10,000 fighting Angels attacked Dublin.

Angel General Jose B., with 10,000 fighting Angels attacked Zaragoza.

Archangel Juanita M.(aka Jenny) with 10,000 fighting Angels attacked Kiev

Angel General Bert M., with 10,000 fighting Angels attacked Moscow.

Archangel Aladdin K., with 10,000 fighting Angels attacked Palermo.

Angel General Carlos B., with 10,000 fighting Angels attacked Belgrade.

Angel General Johnny D., with 10,000 fighting Angels attacked Athens.

Angel Generals Johannes Maximus, Gen. George L., and Gen. Junior D., with 180,000 fighting Angels, pressed the attacked on all other evil forces in Europe. Their additional duty included providing reinforcements to other Angel units in Europe as needed.

The battle for Europe was tremendous and lasted 3 months. 80,000 fighting Angels were wounded. These wounded Angels were sent to Heaven immediately for needed healing services. All these wounded Angels were placed in the Light and Love of God and provided protection by Michael the Archangel and his forces.

112 Million devils, demons, demon hounds, and evil Souls were defeated and destroyed without mercy.

The Angels of Light and Love Penny R., Judy S., Sandy M., and Carey G., were able to save 87 million devils and evil Souls and bring these back to Light and Love of **God**.

At the end of the Battle for Europe, **Archangel Bridget D.,** Angel **Gen. Esteban B**., and **Gen. Johannes Maximus** announced to **God** that Europe was now pacified and all of Europe was now in the hands of **God** and permanently a part of Heaven.

Chapter Twenty seven - Let the fight on Earth begin - Africa

Anxiously waiting for the fight to begin, the forces of Angels in Africa immediately jumped into the Frey as soon as July 10th at 6pm GMT **God's** illuminating light made the evil forces in Africa glow red as well stopping their movement or communication among themselves.

In Africa, the issues were magnified in that no one city was of special concern, but the entire country would have to be assessed for battle. The Angel forces in Africa were as ready as ever to bring the fight to all evil forces in Africa so when on July 10th at 6 pm GMT **God's** light illuminated Africa, the fight to liberate Africa from all evil began. The assignments went as follows:

Archangel Ashley L., 20,000 fighting Angels attacked Somalia.

Angel General Teo M., with 20,000 fighting Angels attacked Egypt.

Archangel Catherine L,. with 20,000 fighting Angels attacked Libya.

Angel General Chuck K., with 20,000 fighting Angels attacked Sudan.

Archangel Sarah L. with 20,000 fighting Angels attacked both Congo.

Angel General Roger R., with 20,000 fighting Angels attacked Angola.

Angel General Terry S., with 20,000 fighting Angels attacked So. Africa.

Angel Generals Bill M., and Zack, with 74,000 fighting Angels attacked the remaining countries in Africa not yet covered. In addition, these two generals were to supply fighting Angels to any area of Africa requesting assistance.

The battle for Africa lasted 6 weeks and cost 47,000 Angel casualties. As per instructions, the wounded Angels were immediately transported to Heaven for healing and rest under the protection and love of God.

73 million devils, demons, demon hounds, and evil Souls were completely and utterly destroyed.

The Angels of Light and Love, Heather O., Janet M., and Lara M., were able to save and restore to the Light and Love of God 104 million devils, demons, and evil Souls who preferred the love of **God** over anything Hell had to offer.

At the end of the battle for Africa, **Archangel Ashley L.,** and **Angel General Teo M.,** declared to **God** that all of Africa and Madagascar were now in **God's** hands and a permanent a part of Heaven.

CHAPTER TWENTY EIGHT - LET THE FIGHT ON EARTH BEGIN - ASIA

In Asia, like in Africa, the issues of concern for the Angel force of the continent of Asia were that the entire country must be addressed and not just a single city in that country. Therefore, **Michael the Archangel** informed **Angel General Carlos II** and **Archangel Camille H.**, that the fighting forces in Asia were increased from the original 234,000 to 284,000, an additional 50,000 fighting Angels. Also, 2 Angel Generals (Michael A., and Angel R,) and one Archangel (Angelica R.E.) will be added to the forces. The changes were immediately approved and this increase of forces was forwarded to Angel General Richard W., and Angel General Paul H.G. Knowing this, when God's light illuminated the Asia continent, the battle scene and force allotment to defeat evil in Asia was divided as follows:

Archangel Richard W., with 40,000 fighting Angels attacked China.

Archangel Susanna W. with 20,000 fighting Angels attacked Cambodia.

Archangel Andrew M. with 20,000 fighting Angels attacked Pakistan.

Archangel Paul H.G. with 20,000 fighting Angels attacked India.

Archangel Angelica R.E. with 20,000 fighting Angels attacked Japan.

Angel General Michael A. with 30,000 fighting Angels attacked N. Korea.

Angel General Angel R. with 30, 000 fighting Angels attacked Viet Nam.

Angel General Eddie R. with 20,000 fighting Angels attacked Philippines.

Angel General Chucky R. with 20,000 fighting Angels attacked Malaysia.

Angel Generals Ric O., Ken and Olga U. with 54,000 fighting Angels attacked the other areas of Asia not yet covered.

The battle for Asia lasted 2 months and cost 98,000 Angel casualties. Help was required to transport that many Angels to Heaven where care and Rest awaited them in the arms of **God** and the forces of Heaven.

140 million devils, demons, demon hounds, and evil Souls were demolished and forever destroyed.

The Angels of Light and Love Caleb R., Carter R. (the Bombones brothers), Andrea O., and Teresa A., gave God the good news that 250 million devils, demons, and evil Souls in Asia were saved and awaited God's Love and Forgiveness.

The Archangel Paul H.G., Archangel Richard W,. and Angel General Michael A. were proud to announce to God that all of Asia was rid of all evil and can now be a part of Heaven.

CHAPTER TWENTY NINE - LET THE FIGHT ON EARTH BEGIN - AUSTRALIA AND NEW ZEALAND.

The battle for Australia and New Zealand would take place as a whole country with no city singled out to be attacked separately. On July 10th at 6 pm GMT, as soon as the light of **God** spread it's illumination over Australia and New Zealand, the Earth forces began the attack on all evil in their respective areas of assignments:

Angel General Arty M., with 10,000 fighting Angels attacked New Zealand.

Archangel Vicki C. with 20,000 fighting Angels attacked North Australia.

Archangel Larry J with 20,000 fighting Angels attacked Southern Australia.

Angel General Amy H. with 20,000 fighting Angels attacked Western Australia.

Archangel Lisa H. with 20,000 fighting Angels attacked Eastern Australia.

The battle for Australia and New Zealand lasted 3 weeks with 18,000 Angels suffering wounds or injuries. These Angels were immediately transported to Heaven for care and rest, as well as being back in the Light and Love of **God** and his protection,.

1 million devils, demons, demon hounds and evil Souls were destroyed in fierce hand to hand combat.

The Angels of Light and Love Joann R. and Sylvia R. were able to save

7 million devils, demons, and evil Souls who without pressure, wanted to return to the love and protection of **God**.

At the end of the battle, Angel General Arty and Archangel Alexis, with extreme pride in their chest, proclaimed to **God** that Australia and New Zealand were now rid of all evil and can now be considered a part of **God's** Heaven.

CHAPTER THIRTY - LET THE FIGHT ON EARTH BEGIN - ANTARCTICA

God held no illusions that Antarctica contained its share of evil. Many evil entities for thousands of years tried to hide in the cold wastelands. A small but potent Angel force was allocated in the plan to rid Earth of all evil. At 6pm GMT, God illuminated Antarctica with his brilliant light. The light so warm and filled with his love that the ice began to melt. Lucky for Antarctica, the light lasted only two minutes. Immediately, the forces of Antarctica began their attack. Antarctica was divided into 3 distinct sections. (right, center, and left).

Angel General Kevin N. with 18,000 fighting Angels attacked the left section.

Archangel David S. with 18,000 fighting Angels attacked the center section.

Angel General Scott N. with 18,000 fighting Angels attacked the right section.

The battle for Antarctica lasted 2 weeks with the Angel force suffering 6,000 wounded or injured. These wounded Angels, as per plan, were immediately transported to Heaven for care and protection from God and the forces of Heaven.

300,000 devils, demons, demon hounds and evil Souls were destroyed.

The Angel of Light and Love Maria A, was able to convert 700,000 devils and evil Souls.

At the end of the battle, **Archangel David S. and Gen. Scott N.**, proclaimed to **God** that Antarctica was clear of all evil and was now a part of Heaven.

CHAPTER THIRTY ONE - END OF THE BATTLE FOR EARTH - GOD PROCLAIMS VICTORY ON EARTH

The entire battle for Earth, the battle to rid, once and for all, the evil that had infested and permeated throughout the world, lasted nearly four months of difficult and horrendous fighting.

In proclaiming victory on Earth, **God** thanked all the forces on Heaven and Earth that made the victory possible. **God,** in honoring the victory, noted the following statistics:

240,000 fighting Angels were wounded or injured. No deaths.

358,300,000 devils, demons, demon hounds, and evil Souls were destroyed.

The statistics that caused celebration in the heart of **God** as well as in the hearts of all others in Heaven was the following statistics.

533,700,000 devils and evil Souls converted from evil and pledged allegiance and service to God and to all the Angels in Heaven and Earth.

Over 500 million Souls were returned to the Love and Light of God.

"Halleluiah"!

The next important step in securing Earth was to ensure that all the Souls committed into the Sea awaiting **God's** call to return to Heaven was carried out. **God** entrusted **Archangel of Light Tomas O.** and **Archangel of Love Carla O.** to oversee this project. After cleansing all the Seas and waterways of all evil, 15 million additional happy Souls were returned from the Seas and placed once more in **God's** loving hands.

With all the continents and their surrounding land and Seas cleared of all evil, **God** proclaimed that Earth was now a true part of Heaven, and as such,

No evil can ever enter Earth, now or any time in the future. After God' proclamation, any person or Soul who tries to embrace evil in any way, will automatically and immediately disintegrate, never to feel God's love again.

All of the Earth Angels involved in the fight to defeat evil on Earth, were given permission to return to their homes and their prior lives. Each of these Angels was to retain their Angel titles as well as their Angel wings. The remaining fighting Angels from Heaven, who were sent to Earth by God, were reordered to assist Angel General Augusto L. and those Angels guarding the entrances and exits gates of Hell.

The fight to destroy Hell was about to begin.

CHAPTER THIRTY TWO - LET THE FIGHT IN TO DESTROY PERDITION BEGIN - PRELIMINARY ACTIONS

In planning for the fight on Earth, **God** and all his advisors also looked at the fight to destroy evil thus destroying Hell. The point being that once the attacked on Earth began, Lucifer and his forces would know about the combat and try to send help to the evil forces now on Earth.

To prevent the forces of Hades from doing so, **God** and Michael the Archangel proposed the following:

On July 10th, one minute prior to 6pm GMT, when **God's** brilliant light flashed, all the entrances and exits to and from Hell would be closed shut, allowing no light, noise, or communication to pass by these gates. All of Hades would be shut off and blind as to what was happening on Earth. **God** made sure that under no circumstances any leaks or information about the attack on Earth would be known to Lucifer and his forces. Since the battle for Earth lasted nearly 4 months, **God** insisted on tight security, strict discipline, and strong forces at each of the entrances and exits. In addition, the following force will be deployed.

At the end of the battle for Africa, **Archangel Ashley L.** will return all of her remaining fighting Angels to **Angel General Esmeraldo L.** at exit gate number one (Mogadishu, Somalia). These fighting Angels will assist to keep exit gate number one completely shut until the battle for Hell begins and **Angel General Esmeraldo L.** under **God's** orders, opens the gate.

When the battle in Asia is completed, Angel **General Angel R.** will bring his remaining fighting Angels to **Angel General Richard O.**, at exit gate number 2 (Hanoi, N. Vietnam) and help keep the gate shut completely until Angel General Richard O., under orders from **God**, opens the gate.

When the battle for North America is completed, **Angel General Carlos II** will bring his remaining fighting Angels to **Angel General Juan L. (Ponce)** at exit gate number 3. The forces will help keep the gate shut until **Angel General Juan L.** gets the order from **God** to open the gates.

At the completions of the battle for Earth, all fighting Angels not yet assigned will report to **Angel General Augusto L.** to help keep the 7 entrances to Hell shut until **God** gives the order to open the gates, begin the attack and destroy Hell.

CHAPTER THIRTY THREE - LUCIFER GETS NERVOUS

After the first day when all the gates, both in and out of Hell, were shut tight, Lucifer began to suspect that his new exits from Hell had been discovered. He also believed that the forces of Heaven must be playing war games at the gates, which Heaven had done on many prior occasions.

Activities in Hell continued with the torture and abuse of the poor Souls that resided in Hell. The joy of punishment for these Souls continued for the devils and demons whose job it was to torment and cause grief to the Souls.

On the second day of shutdown, Lucifer noted that he had not heard from any of his many devils and demons on Earth. Lucifer also noted that no new Souls were being sent to Hell for torture. This lack of action began to prey in Lucifer's mind. "Let Heaven play its game at the gates, I just don't care and I got all eternity to wait" said Lucifer.

After one week, all the devils and demons in Hades began to communicate among themselves that something big was happening outside the gates of Hell and that something big was coming to Hell. Lucifer noted their murmurs and for some strange reason, Lucifer felt nervous himself.

This was not normal. Heaven always had new Souls to send to Hell and Hell was always ready to receive them. Something is very wrong, very wrong.

At the end of ten days, Lucifer called his devil council together. "We have a huge problem facing us at this time" stated Lucifer.. The minor devils and demons were getting frustrated at not getting new Souls to torment. The current Souls could only be given the same tortured to a point, after which, the torture was less effective and the Souls would know what to expect next, demeaning the value of the torture. "We have to break the blockade on our gates at all cost", stated Lucifer. I want the following military action to take place immediately. One army consisting of 5,000 mean and unforgiving devils to push its way through **exit gate** number 1 and open that gate. Another army consisting of 7,000 mean and cruel devils will force open the **entrance gate** 1. When these gates are opened, the devils are to attack and destroy any Angels around the gates and immediately commence communications with the devils on Earth. When these objectives are reached, a concise report was to be given to Lucifer for his evaluation.

CHAPTER THIRTY FOUR - LUCIFER'S FIRST DISAPPOINTMENT.

Lucifer was livid. When he spoke His voice was like a dragon with a painful foot. He could not believe what his devils where reporting to Him. After having centuries of events going his way, now was not the time to get blocked at every turn. Something bad was happening to the place where "bad" was the norm.

The two armies sent to open two of the gates utterly failed and were completely scattered and left running for cover and distance from what met them at the gates. There were no words to explain what they saw or what made them desert their assignments. Never before has this many devils failed in their assignments. Lucifer's skin began to crawl, reminding him that the last time His skin crawled this way was when He was defeated in His attempt to overthrow **God** and the forces of Heaven. Why was He getting this feeling now? How strange. How very strange.

After his forces failure to open some of the gates of Hell, Lucifer decided that perhaps there was a good reason for the gates of Hades being shut tight.

Perhaps another fight to take over Heaven and defeat God was underway at this very moment. It would explain why no new Souls were being sent to Hell. It would also explain why the gates where secured so tightly, preventing the defeated forces of Heaven to escape into Hell.

Lucifer accepted this theory for the bad events that had taken place and for any further bad events that would take place until Heaven was defeated. Knowing that whomever was doing the fighting, after achieving victory over **God**, would elevate Lucifer to King of Heaven and Hell. Lucifer began to feel his normal self again. Nothing could stop him now from reaching his true dream. NOTHING.

Lucifer ordered his forces to stand down and enjoy the rest. He ordered that the Underworld be made ready to celebrate. A new order and ruler of Heaven and Hell was to be crowned shortly and Lucifer would be the recipient of that title.

The torture and tormenting of the Souls would stop for now, At the celebration, torturing would begin again with fervor. Lucifer's skin no longer crawled with anxiousness. All was fine again. He felt great.

Chapter Thirty five - Surprise, surprise, surprise.

On November 11th, at 7 am GMT, **God** gave the order to open all the 7 entrances to Perdition and begin the attack on Hell. **God** wanted the 3 exits from Hell kept shut for the present moment to allow the surprised devils a chance to flee and flood Inferno7, causing Infernal 7 to be over crowded with more devils than Inferno 7 was designed for, I.e., causing confusion and disorder. Since all the 7 entrance to Hades enter and end in Inferno one, all 7 Angel Generals, Archangels, and fighting Angels entered in Infernal one at the same time. At 7 am, the first thing that happened after the 7 entrance gates were open, a tremendous white flash of light preceded the fighting forces. These extremely bright lights came from the Angels of Light that accompanied the fighting forces of Heaven. The light temporarily blinded the devils on guard at the gates while other devils, not at the gates, believed the lights were part of the celebration they have been told to expect. None of these devils were expecting trouble and therefore took no military action until the forces of Heaven were on top of them. (Surprise!)

Leading Angel General Augusto L. upon entering Inferno one, began to look for the leaders of the devils in order to overtake them in battle. **Angel of Light Josefina**, was able to illuminate several leaders and Augusto L. charged into them with fury and anger for the pain that they had caused these Souls. One leader, a large lizard like man, with claws like komodo dragons, charged at Augusto L. The fight was fierce, one on one, no holds barred. After 5 minutes of furious fighting, Gen. Augusto L. knocked this devil down mortally wounded on the slippery floor, whereupon his death, disintegrated right in front of Augusto L. eyes. The remaining forces of Augusto L., utilizing the additional forces arriving in Inferno one, furiously attacked the remaining devils, demons, and demon hounds of Inferno one. A second devil leader approached Augusto L., thrusting a dirty, rusty spear at him. Augusto parried the spear and with a powerful downward swing of his sword, terminated the devil and his attack. The fighting continued and any wounded Angel was transported to Heaven by **Archangel Ramon**, the transportation coordinator. Within hours, Inferno one was defeated. This victory, Augusto L., proudly reported to **God**.

Chapter Thirty six - Lots of guts but no glory.

With Inferno one saturated with all of the Angel forces who attacked Hell at the same time, the evil forces of Inferno one were overwhelmed and truly were no match for the Heavenly forces. The devil force of Inferno one were rendered useless. After just a few hours of fighting, the forces of Inferno one were decimated and in disarray. With nearly ¾ of their forces destroyed, the evil forces could not command the Souls or continue the torment of these unfortunate Souls in Inferno one. The Souls began to escape their captors and run towards the Angels of Light for protection.

During the fighting, 99 % of the Souls in Hell one got on their knees and begged for forgiveness. Working with efficiency of hard practice, the Angels of Light and Love were able to treat and convert to God, 16 million Souls who were waiting for classification and punishment. The one percent of Souls that did not request forgiveness were immediately destroyed along with the rest of the evil forces of Inferno one.

All of the demon hounds and almost all of the demons and devils were destroyed in the battle in Inferno one. Only 148 devils were converted to the Light and Love of **God** while 8 million devils and demons were destroyed without mercy. Being that the devils and demons of Inferno one loved their job of torturing new Souls in Hell, absolutely no quarters were offered them. When looking back on the battlefield of Inferno one, A warrior Angel stated "this looks like Jones Town, only a million times as gruesome."

The torture instruments used in Inferno one were destroyed by the **Archangel Joe T. and Archangel Edwin M.**, who volunteered to destroy all of the torture equipment used in Hell. It was understood by God, that after these two Archangels destroyed the torture equipment, no one on Heaven or Earth could recognize where the pieces came from or to where the pieces belonged to. A total of 6 million torture machines were destroyed in Inferno one.

Inferno one will remain under the protection of Angel General Augusto L. and a small contingent of fighting Angels. A safe base camp will be established on Inferno one to include 16 medical field hospitals, 4 square miles of clean flat area for holding Souls to be converted to the Light and Love of **God**, and 1 square mile to hold Souls and injured Angels for transportation to Heaven. One Archangel quoted " the devils in Inferno one spilled their guts, but got no glory".

Chapter Thirty seven - Lucifer's becomes unstable.

The instant that Inferno one was attacked, Lucifer felt that someone had betrayed him. How could Heaven keep a secret that long? Why had not one devil on Earth escape to give him warning? What was **God** offering to his devils and the Souls to stop fighting? Nothing was making any sense. Within just a few hours, Inferno one, his strong hold and first stop in Hell for all Souls, was defeated and the devils that survive were running backwards in fear and cowardice. Lucifer felt that he could no longer trust anyone. He became remorse, despondent, and angry. Somebody was going to pay for their lapse in security. For their lapse in integrity. "Hell", someone was going to pay. Pay real big. At any minute, the forces of Heaven would be attacking any or all other levels of His Abyss. Lucifer sensed that no matter what was happening on Earth, there is certainly a war going on in Hell. What could He do with few or no one to trust. Was he abandoned?

Lucifer's body guards, feeling their master's pain, took Lucifer to the side and express to Him that regardless of the circumstances in Inferno one, Lucifer was a trained general himself, and there was still a strong devil force available to him that could devastate any force that **God** could throw against him. Lucifer, they told him boldly, you will be fighting in your home grounds, and that is an advantage you have and one advantage that **God** would not expect of you. The words that the body guard spoke were like an aspirin, relieving his pain and restoring his faith in himself and his forces.

In addressing his remaining devils, demons, and demon hounds, Lucifer, by his mere presence as Hell's greatest leader, managed to fill the devils with encouragement and fighting spirit. With his despondency in the back of his mind, Lucifer ordered all of Hades forces to fight to the death or until the forces attacking Hell were defeated. He stated "we will win, and we will establish a new Hell here and on Earth. Be mindful of your sacrifices and to whom you owe allegiance for giving you the power to torture and punish Souls in Hell. Don't let me down. I will be fighting at your sides at all times. Never surrender. Remember, you are the best fighters in the whole universe."

As Inferno one crumbled before Him, Lucifer, forgetting Himself, said a little prayer for victory in Hell and the defeat of **God** and his forces.

CHAPTER THIRTY EIGHT - HOW DO YOU STOP A STEAM ROLLER?

With Inferno two being his area of responsibility, and after helping Angel General Augusto L. defeat Inferno one, **Angel General Eduardo L., (aka Eddie)** and his **Angel of Light Jaime**, wasted no time in pressing the battle to the devil force in Inferno two that came up to meet their advances.

With Angel of Light Jaime illuminating his way, General Eddie swiftly cleared a path with his powerful sword, primed in Heaven with the special ingredients primed by **God**.

Up to meet him in combat, three devils, with large heads resembling that of an alligator with fangs so sharp that they could cut iron. Their arms were 5 feet long with sharp claws. These demons had the ability to fly and spit fire. Their feet resembled those found on T-Rex lizards. They were considered the "Bullies" of all of the Nether world. They were smiling as they flew into battle.

General Eddie, who also had wings and could fly, spread his battle wings showing magnificent, beautiful, and pure white feathers, that when fully extended reached 100 feet on both sides of his body. Flying up to meat the first devil, Eddie swooped under him and penetrated its defenses and before the devil could react, Eddie cut his wings and terminated his life. The 2nd flying devil tried to outflank Eddie, but with training fit to be a "top gun fighter" Eddie outmaneuvered him and in a flash of unbelievable speed, caused severe turbulence under his wings to deflect the attack and place Eddie right behind the 2nd devil. With his bow and arrows, Eddie shot 7 treated arrows into the devil's, killing the 2nd devil while in flight. The 3rd flying devil, seeing the flying ability of Eddie, tried to bring the fight to the ground, but even there, Eddie, a trainer of Fighting Angels in sword combat, was able to over come his third opponent. General Eddie's forces continued to press the attack. With his forces, and the forces sent to assist him, Angel General Eddie had completely scattered or defeated all the demon hounds, and 97 percent (8.2 million) of the devil force in Inferno two. His forces managed to save 7 million Souls who requested to be forgiven and returned to the light and Love of **God**. A fighting Angel noted that for all their bullying, these supposedly strong devils were squashed flat, just as if they were steam rolled. Lucifer was livid at the news of his loses. Lucifer was proud that at least the devils in Hell two went down fighting.

CHAPTER THIRTY NINE - WHAT YOU DON'T KNOW CAN HURT YOU.

After two days of fighting, two levels of Hades have been defeated. Lucifer, trying to discover a military solution to stop the advances, decided that the way to stop the advances and win the war was to order his forces to inflict so many injuries and casualties to the Angel forces that **God** would not be able to sustain the loses and retreat out of Hell before all his Angels are destroyed.

Lucifer did Not know that on Inferno one 16 field hospitals were established to create a quick repair of the injuries and a transportation system set up to quickly bring reinforcements or to return the previously injured Angels back to the battle. Lucifer also did not know that a million fighting Angels were being held in reserve just to relieve the injured until they could return to the battle. The Angel forces fighting in Hell would never diminish, but would grow stronger. Lucifer did not know that **God**, with all his powers, proclaimed the no Angel would die in the war to defeat Hell. Lucifer could not be aware that his pitiful solution to win the war was never to succeed.

Lucifer's battle intelligence could only give him restricted information. Not being able to look back into Inferno two or Inferno one, the devils did not know that at each of these two levels, the Angel forces kept only a small detachment of fighting Angels and then released the rest of their fighting force to the next General leading the attack on the next level of Hell.

Due to Hell's set-up, an invading force would have to cross over the bridges and fight one level at a time.

What the devils in Hell did not comprehend was that in making the defense of Hell one level at a time, the attacking forces could send to battle more troops than the evil troops protecting each level of Hell. This defense would not be sustainable for very long before the forces in each level was overwhelm with superior numbers of combatants.

The forces of Heaven, being aware of the situation, used this fact to their advantage. With 5 more levels of Hell to be conquered, each Angel General knew what was expected of him and his troops. The fighting so far has been furious, deadly, and without let-up. **On to Inferno three.**

"An angel of light, love and healing attending to an injured
angel during the fight for Earth and the fight to end Hell."

CHAPTER FORTY - WEAPONS MAKE THE DIFFERENCE.

Angel General Harry L. could feel the tension and the pressure of the battle. He felt them very clearly and he knew that tension and pressure in battle could be a friend if handled properly. Lucky for Him, the Angel of light he was given was no amateur, but an experienced Angel that has been in over 100 combat mission. His **Angel of Light was Juan-Jose L.**

Upon crossing the bridges from Inferno two to Inferno three, Gen. Harry L. noted that two sets of armies where sent to meet him in combat. The devil force from Inferno three as well as the half the devil force from Inferno four. Angel of Light Juan-Jose smiled because he enjoyed helping his generals in battle. Let them come, we are ready for them. The strategy employed by the devils were to kill or injure the Angel leaders so that the other Angels would be confused.

Besides Gen. Harry's own Angel force, additional tens of thousand additional fighting Angels were added to his command from the forces of other Angel Generals that were waiting to attack their level of responsibility.

As in the two previous levels of Hell, the Angels with superior weapons that only needed to nick an opponent to cause death, sliced into the on-coming devils combatants with a lust for combat and the knowledge that their fight and cause was just and blessed by God.

With Angel of Light Juan-Jose lighting the way, Gen. Harry met the first devils in combat. These devils were a 2 headed beast with yellow glowing eyes that never left his victims out of his sight. These devils were short but very wide and fast. They had long arms, each carrying a spear or a sword.

Meeting them head on, Gen. Harry was able to slide under the first one and

As he passed underneath, cut off three of its four legs. At the instant he got off the floor, another devil tried to pin him down, but Angel of Light Juan-Jose temporarily blinded him and allowed Gen. Harry to defeat him in one to one combat. The battle continued for hours upon hours, but by the end of the day, Gen. Harry had won the fight. With Juan-Jose at his side, Gen. Harry proclaimed to God that 6 million Souls were save and converted back to his love. 9.5 million devils were destroyed. There were now three levels of Hell in **God's** control.

CHAPTER FORTY-ONE - NEVER SPLIT YOUR FORCES

Lucifer suspected that Inferno four was now in trouble. With half of it's fighting force decimated while assisting Inferno three, there was not much to do but to hope that the forces of Heaven had suffered so many injuries that **God** might call a truce or even surrendered before attacking Inferno four. That was not to be. **Angel General Petr O.**, and **Angel of Light Kris O.**, commenced their attack immediately, not giving the devils on Inferno four a chance to re-group or be re-enforced with further troops. Quickly spreading over each corner of Inferno four, Gen. Petr's troop engaged the depleted forces opposing them in Inferno four. Gen. Petr, leading his troops, located several devils hiding to ambush his troops. Faster than a hurricane on skates, Gen. Petr went hand to hand with the first devil he found. This devil was at least 12 feet tall, muscular, with teeth that look like they came from a great white shark. The devil was trying to stomp on Gen. Petr, but his Angel of Light Kris, deflected and confused the devil by shining her light of Love into his Technicolor glowing eyes. The quick move by Angel of Light Kris, gave Gen. Petr enough time to avoid the stomp attempt and commence with his own attack on this devil. While the devil was distracted, Gen. Petr struck with his spear in an upward, 45 degree angle, catching the devil by surprise and ending the fight. The devil then disintegrated into dust. The other devils who where in hiding, began to flee but were engaged in battle by other members of Gen. Petr's troops. Although the battle with these giant devils was fierce, the superior number of Angel troops overwhelmed the devils in Inferno four in just a matter of 4 hours. Most of the time was wasted in trying to catch the fleeing devils.

Gen. Petr O. and his Angel of Light Kris O. were proud to express to God, that Inferno four was no long a part of Hell. Only 3 million devils, demons, and devil hounds were destroyed. Fortunately, 9 million more Souls were saved and requested **God's** forgiveness. These Souls were transported to Inferno one holding area by Archangel Ramon, for further processing in cleansing their Souls. The Archangels Joe T. and Edwin M., after following the victories in four levels of Hell, reported to God that up to this point they've destroyed a total of 35 million torture equipment and instruments.

CHAPTER FORTY-TWO - HIT AND RUN.

Lucifer still believed that a victory was not only possible, but would more than likely occur on Inferno six. Lucifir instructed his devils in Inferno five to fight ferously and to cause the Angel army as many casualties as possible, then when the damage to **God's** forces was completed, they should escape into Inferno six and prepare to scatter the forces of **God**.

Angel General Esmeraldo B. and his Angel of Light Santiago B., were assigned by **God** and Michael the Archangel to defeat Lucifer's forces at Inferno five. **God**, with his consults of Angel Generals and Archangels, and **Jesus**, informed Gen. Esmeraldo B. to expect a "hit and run" situation and not to fall for their trap. Gen. Esmeraldo B., an expert in hand to hand fighting, and who trained his troops in this art of fighting, accepted the advise of the consuls and prepared to go into battle.

Facing Gen. Esmeraldo B. were mean looking devils that had bodies of beluga whales with long arms that had a large lobster claw on each end. Their heads were large and scaly with mouth and teeth that resemble those of a barracuda fish. Mean looking, did I say? Plunging into battle, Gen. Esmeraldo B. formed 15 seven by seven deep line of fighting Angels. This formation cause the devils in Inferno five to scatter unable to penetrate the tight fighting formation. Behind each formation were 2,000 archers that each could send 100 arrows a minute into their area of combat. Devils caught inbetween lines were quickly attacked without any mercy. Gen. Esmeraldo B., catching a devil leader trying to infiltrate the lines, threw the devil over his back and before the devil was able to get back on his feet, sliced both lobster claws off and eliminated his opponent. The devil disintegrated.

The rest of the devils in Inferno five, believing that a large amount of damage was done to the Angel forces, escaped into Inferno six leaving all the Souls and the torture equipment behind. Actually, Very few of Gen. Esmeraldo B.'s fighting Angels were actually injured in the fight for Inferno five. Only 46,000 devils, demons, and devil hounds were destroyed. 11 million Souls were saved and placed in the loving hands of God. Proudly, Gen. Esmeraldo B. proclaimed that Inferno five is no longer a part of Hell.

CHAPTER FORTY-THREE - DESPERATION SETS IN.

Lucifer pushed aside the feeling of some of his fighting devils that no matter what type of force was used against the forces of **God**, no penetration or stopping of their armies was forth coming. Lucifer felt that he was still in control of the situation and did not let the frustation of his underling enter his mind. When the exits of Hell were opened, the forces of Hades would trap the forces of God between Inferno Seven and Inferno one. Inferno six was home to some of his most dangerous and serious fighting devils. The forces of **God**, if not destroyed at this level, would certainly suffer a great amount of grave casualties. His Gargolyes and shift changing devils will be difficult to stop or defeated. Just let the forces of **God** enter. We will see how many of them leave.

Army General "Mr. Gabriel" A. and his Angel of Light Sofia were designated by **God** to handle the devil forces on Inferno six. Gen. "Mr. Gabriel" A., Knowing he would be facing flying demons as well as shift changing devils, trained his forces in both air to air and air to ground combat. Gen. Mr. Gabriel, knowing the strengths of his forces, charged into Inferno six with his wings spread wide open, Each of his wings were 45 feet long and 8 feet wide. A ninety foot wingspan. The wings were of pure white feathers that glowed with a kiss of sunshine. The purity of the feathers memorized any devil or demon that gazed upon them. All of his fighting force had lovely wings with spands of 30 feet. The first devil Mr. Gabriel met in battle was a 12 foot devil that had an elongated mouth full of teeth that ooze meanness from every tooth. The devils head was full of green spiky hair. His eyes glowed with evilness. There were four horns on top of the devil's head that he attempted to ram and gore Mr. Gabriel without success. With swift up and down movements, Mr. Gabriel was able to avoid being puncture by the horns. Now facing this devil, Mr. Gabriel faked a thrust of is spear causing the devil to move to the side and attempt a swing with his sword. Unfortunately for the devil, Mr. Gabriel was expecting the move and paried the sword downward and instantly slice upward with his own sword. The movement caught the devil by surprise and stunned, was not able to move away from Mr. Gabriel's sword that terminated its life. Angel of Light Sofia illuminated the entire fight. The devil that was just defeated by Mr. Gabriel was the toughs and strongest of all the devils in Inferno six. His defeat so quickly totally demoralized the fighting forces on Inferno six. Desperation set in causing the remaining devils to scatter and flee into Inferno seven. A total of 10 million Souls were captured and return to the Grace and Love of God. Hell six was no longer a part of Hell. Lucifer overestimated his powers. (3 million devils died in Inferno six.

CHAPTER FORTY-FOUR - NO WHERE TO RUN, NO WHERE TO HIDE.

Lucifer was livid and demanded loyalty from his escaped and massing devils. Inferno seven was over crowded with the forces that retreated from prior level of Hell that were defeated by **God's** forces. Stationed at Inferno six were so many fighting Angels awaiting to attack Inferno seven that not one of Lucifer's devil leaders could count or estimate the forces posed to attacked them. Only they knew that it was a hell of a large number prepared to attack them. So far, the three exits from Hell had not be opened, and this gave Lucifer a ray of hope. If He and his forces could escape out of Hell, then **God** would be helpless to try and stop Lucifer from infecting the Earth. This thought gave Lucifer satisfaction. Still, He thought He had a strong demonic force at each other level of hell but they were defeated or scattered back to Inferno seven. He knew He had his own fighting devils on Inferno seven that He had hand picked for their ferousity and staying power. He also had 100 Fallen Angels that were worth 100 armies each. Perhaps, just perhaps the fight with **God** will end here and He will still be king of Heaven and Earth. Yes, Lucifer felt much better. Lucifer called in his Fallen Angels and all of the remaining leaders of his demonic force, and began to plan a counter attack on the Angel forces waiting on Inferno six and at the same time, try again to open the exits from Inferno seven. This time he would succeed. No failing now.

Lucifer noted that **God's** forces made it so that He nor his devils had no where to run, and no where to hide. Still, Lucifer felt that when the fighting starts, it would be **God** with no place to run. None the less, Lucifer was not going to run. He would fight to the end and in doing so, he would come out the winner.

The Angel forces on Inferno six were waiting patiently for word to begin their attack. The Angel General scheduled to enter Hell seven would be **Angel General John Richard M. and his Angel of Light Saul C.** Their forces, combined with the forces released to them from the conquered levels of Hell, will lead the fight and block any devil's attempt to escape from Inferno seven. At this moment, all six prior levels of hell were in God's control with all remaining devils blocked in Inferno seven.

Already the devils from the other levels of Hell were jealous of the goodies and looks that the devils on Hell seven enjoyed. Their jealousy lead to fighting and pushing among themselves. Lucifer contemplated that never in the history of Hell, has an invading army caused so much destruction and disarray in Hell, Even causing the devils to fight among themselves.

CHAPTER FORTY-FIVE - WHERE DID I GO WRONG?

The stage was set. All of **God's** forces were primed and ready. Lucifer and his armies were pinned down on Inferno seven with no room to stretch without bumping into another devil.

God sent word with an emissary, I.e., a captured devil leader, to notify all the devil forces in Inferno seven to refuse to fight and get on their knees when the fighting started. The forces of **God** will give them a chance to pledge allegiance to **God** and be returned to Heaven with all the Glory and Love of **God**. All devils and demons who refused the offer would be terminated on the spot. Lucifer, in his anger, demolished the emissary in front of his forces. "Any one else wants to quit fighting?" Inferno seven was suddenly very quiet.

Unbeknown to Lucifer and his forces, the 100 Fallen Angels decided that they had enough of what Lucifer and Hell had to offer them. They remembered how beautiful and peaceful Heaven was and how they were respected as Archangels in **God's** Heaven. These 100 Fallen Angels decided that they wanted to return to the Light and Love of **God**, and so they enclosed themselves in a meeting room in Lucifer's palace with 3,000 additional devils that also wanted to be in **God's** Light. Here, in this meeting room, they waited for the forces of Heaven to find and rescue them.

"God gave the word attack and end Lucifer's reign of terror. Destroy Hell".

While the devils and Lucifer were preparing their attack to break the strangle hold, Angel General John Richard M. and his Angel of Light Saul C, crossed the bridges from Inferno six to Inferno seven and opened up with 20,000 flying arrows that were aimed at the center of the devil's rank and concentration. No sooner than the arrows took flight, General John Richard and his Angel of Light Saul C., gave a rousing rebel yell and 50,000 screaming fighting angels followed him into Inferno seven. Fear and disorder broke among the devils and many devils began a backward stampede. The sudden rush of devils backward cause hundreds of devils to fall beneath the stampeding feet and meet their deaths.

Angel General Esmeraldo L., Angel General Richard O., and Angel General Juan L., aka Ponce, burst open the **3 exits** from Hell and charged into the retreating devils. It was a classic pincer movement. Lucifer and his troops where cleverly trapped. "where did I go wrong", cried Lucifer?

CHAPTER FORTY-SIX - ABANDONED BY MY FALLEN ANGELS

Inferno seven was truly overcrouded. Angel Gen. John Richard M. had no trouble finding opponents. With Saul C. next to him lighting his way, John Richard attacked and killed six of Lucifer's hand picked devils. Saul C. just blinded them with his light and John Richard followed up.

The devil forces were now engaged from the front and from the rear. They had no way to go but to try and stand their ground. Angel arrows and spears came raining down on them like a tropical summer rain that washes everything clean. Very few of the devils could get out of the way. The only way to escape the arrows and spears was to escape into Lucifer's fortified mansion. Lucifer, foreseeing this, ordered his human looking devils to close all the doors to his Mansion, allowing entrance to only devils originally assigned to Hell\\\\Inferno seven. This move of shutting off the mansion, forced the devils on the outside to fight and be destroyed or surrender.

The fight outside of Lucifer's mansion was fierce, non stop hand to hand combat. Swords, spears, and arrows were flying everywhere. The devils on the outside of the mansion had determined to go down figting to the last devil. With the strength of a person who knows he is about to die, the adrenaline flowing inside these devils almost forced a hole through the Angel lines. Too bad, the Angel forces had adrenaline of their own and fought their way back and pushed the devils back towards the mansion.

The scene outside of Lucifer's mansion was pure mayhem. Fighting everywhere, on the ground and in the air. Dead devils were lying in layers on top of each other before disintergrating into dust. Many Angels were seen carrying their wounder comrades back to the medical stations.

Inside His mansion, Lucifer's call for the Fallen Angels to report to him went unanswered. Lucifer knew in his mind that the Fallen Angels had resolved not to fight against the forces of **God**. Lucifer felt abandoned; abandoned by the one force that would assured Him a victory over **God**. Lucifer would need a miracle if He or Hell was to survive.

CHAPTER FORTY-SEVEN - OUT OF OPTIONS

The fighting outside of Lucifer's mansion was still on-going. The fighting Angels holding the upper hand had not yet broken the devils resolve to stop fighting. Gen. John Richard requested assistance from the forces of Gen. Esmeraldo L., which were promptly sent without delay to Gen. John Richard. The additional 7,000 fighting Angels tiped the balance and in a matter of one hour, the devils outside of Lucifer's mansion were completely obliterated. The exhausted Angels on Inferno seven, despite intensive searching, could not locate a single living devil outside of Lucifer's mansion. The only fighting devils in all of what was once Hell were now located inside Lucifer's fortified Mansion.

Gen. Richard O., sent the word out to all other fighting Angels not connected with His forces or the forces of Gen. Esmeraldo L, or Gen. Juan L. to rest and ordered a detachment to capture any devils caught trying to escape out of Lucifer's mansion. Gen. Richard O. was first to break down a barrier on the East side of the mansion. Charging down the hallway, General Richard met a force of 4,000 hand picked human looking devils. These devils were well trained and had no chicken in them. Liking a good fight himself, Gen. Richard O, leading his forces, sliced a hole through the devil's line. Immediately, fighting ensued in every inch of the hallway. When the human like devils were defeated, each one disintegrated on the spot where they fell. Pushing forward, the forces of Gen. Richard O soon worked their way through reaching the end of the hallway where no fighting was taking place. Gen. Richard O, seeing that his forces were holding their own with the devil force, continued down the hallway with most of his troops. Turning down a large corridore that had large rooms for holding meetings, he noticed that about 500 devils were trying to break into a room and that it seemed obviously the occupants of that room, did not want the room to be opened by the devils. With a yell that only a great general can administer. Gen. Richard O. and his Angels charged in military style advances into the 500 devils. After 40 minutes of intensed and frightening fighting, the devils were defeated. Inside that room, Gen. Richard O. found the Fallen Angels with the 3,000 repenting devils. Securing the Fallen Angels and the repented devils, Gen. Richard O reported to **God** that the Fallen Angels were returning to his Graces.

CHAPTER FORTY-EIGHT - SOON GOD'S LIGHT WILL BE SHINING IN HELL.

God and the Heavens where rejoicing with pure delight. **God's** Fallen Angels have returned back to the Love and Grace of **God**. After pledging their full allegiance to God and Heaven, the former fallen Angels were now restored to status of Archangels in training. Despite the war continuing in Hell, **God** was very pleased to have His fallen Angels returned. This was a happy day for every person and Soul on Heaven and on Earth.

Back in Inferno seven, Gen. Juan L. (Ponce) found a way to bypass the moat that contained burning lava, and crashed down the main door on the West side of Lucifier's mansion. Gen. Juan L. was known in Heaven for his never give up fighting attitude. The devils that came to meet Gen. Juan L. were in for a very sad and unforgettable fight.

Nearly 140,000 devils met Gen. Juan L. as he crashed the door down to Lucifer's mansion. With the force of light FROM his Angel of Light Digna Merida, Gen. Juan L. blasted through the initial attempt to block his entry.

With his sword of Light and Truth, Gen. Juan l. gave no quarters to the devils that approached him in combat. The first devil was a well trained devil leader and commanded thousands of devil troops. This devil knew what he could do with a sword and had no fear of meeting anyone in combat. Gen. Juan L. clashed swords with this devil leader and finding himself face to face and sword to sword with this devil, pushed back the devils sword so hard, that devil's own sword impaled itself into the devil causing instant death. How could something like this happen to the third most strongest devil besides Lucifer and his body guards. Other devils expecting their leader to win the fight, became despondent and began loosing their will to fight. Without waiting Gen. Juan L. jumped among them, followed by his troops. After hours and hours of hand to hand combat, the 140,000 devils were destroyed to the devil. It was a horrible scene for the devils, but a welcomed sight for the forces of **God**. Holding the ground, he had captured, Gen. Juan L. reported to God that he noted that Lucifer and the remaining devils are waiting in the center courtyard of the mansion, **Hell was a little brighter**.

CHAPTER FORTY-NINE - LUCIFER AND HIS BODY GUARDS.

Angel General Esmeraldo L., with his Angel of Light Juana O., were given the mission to destroy all remaining devils and prepare Hell for the **arrival of Mallory of the Angels** and **her escorts, Gen. Solrac, Gen. Samot, and Gen. Noel**. Gen. Esmeraldo's mission was of high importance to **God** and if the mission was carried out as planned, the demise of Hell was soon to occur.

Smashing down the doors of the North main entrance into Lucifer's mansion, Gen. Esmeraldo L. brought the might of God and all of heaven with him. Angel of Light Juana O., lighting the path before him, gave Gen. Esmeraldo L. a clear view of where the enemies were and where Lucifer and his body guards were located.

Giving the order to avoid attacking or fighting with Lucifer, Gen. Esmeraldo's army was focused on fighting any devils left alive in the Mansion. Already all the hallways and corridors to and from the courtyard were blocked and guarded by the forces of Gen. Richard O., and Gen. Juan L. Leaving a small detachment of Fighting Angels to ensure that no Angels would attack Lucifer by mistake, Gen. Esmeraldo lead the charge that pushed the devils towards the middle of the yard giving them no place to move. With no mercy shown or given, tens of thousands of arrows and spears rained down upon the devils waiting for combat. The 60,000 devils in the courtyard were dispensed with minor trouble.

Ensuring that there were no devils inside Lucifer's mansion other than Lucifer Himself and His body guards, Gen. Esmeraldo L. and his Angel of Light Juana O., requested that each general report their status as to their mission being completed or if their were still devils to be destroyed.

The Angel Generals of each level of Hell were proud to proclaim that all devils in their area of responsibility were either destroyed or converted back to the Light and Love of **God**. Archangels John T. and Edwin M. reported that all of the eight million torture equipment as well as the giant razor blade were destroyed.

Once the courtyard was cleaned of bodies, Gen. Esmeraldo L. gently requested that Lucifer and his body guards walk with him to the center of the courtyard where Mallory of the Angels and her 3 General escorts were waiting to reveal God's message of hope, love, and forgiveness. The next hour was going to be the most important hour of the entire war with Lucifer and his demonic forces. All eyes were on Lucifer. **The fight for Hell is not over yet.**

Chapter Fifty - Three one on one fights remain.

Lucifer noticed that the other Angel Generals and their armies were staying behind and only three Angels were guarding Mallory of the Angels. The fight could still be won if he could just kill God's messenger and spoil the celebrations in heaven.

Giving the go ahead to attack the messenger, Lucifer lunged towards her followed by his body guards, completely ignoring the Angels that were there to protect her. Only a few feet to go and God's messenger would be history.

Expecting Lucifer to pull this kind of stunt, Gen. Solrac, Gen. Samot, and Gen. Noel stepped in front of Mallory of the Angels and each of these generls took on an opponent. General Esmeraldo L. stood by in case any of the 3 remaining 3 devils were able to defeat the escorts. Samot took on the body guard named Hitler. Noel took on the body guard named Moe. Lucifer was Solrac's meat, holding his full power back knowing that in this fight, Lucifer would not be killed, only captured, so Lucifer could hear God's message. The devil Hitler was a tall, slimy and vicious warrior that Lucifer picked for his merciless handling of Souls on Earth as well as in Hell. He was cruel, ruthless and fearless. He had been involved in over 5,000 hand to hand combats with Angels on Earth, all of them victories. Gen. Samot will be fodder for cannons when he, Hitler, was finish with him. Since Hitler had no weapons, Samot placed his weapons aside and truly took Hitler on Mano a Mano (hand to hand).

Samot's first punch landed squarely on Hitler's lip, causing a vicious split and causing Hitler to taste his own blood. Continuing boxing Hitler, Samot landed several body punches that broke several of Hitler's ribs.

Catching Samot with several rights to the head, Hitler began to feel his victory was at hand. Circuling each other, Samot faked a left jab and when Hitler went to block it, Somat hit him with a powerful right punch that turn the lights off in Hitler's eyes. Hitler went down and rolled over. The onlookers could see that in falling, Hitler broke his neck and died, instantly turning into a big puff of dust. So much for his 5,000 hand to hand combats. Gen. Somat stepped back to relieve Gen. Esmeraldo L. and continue to protect Mallory of the Angels. His two partners were fully engaged in a fight.

CHAPTER FIFTY-ONE - WILL THE DEVILS NEVER LEARNED?

Gen. Noel was fighting the devil named Moe. Moe was Lucifer's body Guard and a relentless hater of God and against all prayer in schools. From her time on Earth, Moe did everything she could to destroy **God** as well as any of the world's government that believed in **God**. Moe was excellent in what she did. Her hate discolored any purity she found on Earth. As a devil, Moe was like 300 tigers. It was rummered that when Lucifer over throws the Heavens, she would be placed in command of all the devils in Hell. This devil had a lot to fight for. It was know in Hell that fighting Moe would be suicide three time over. She was muscular with razor sharp nails that were 3 inches long and harder than steel. Her toes carried 4 inch long toe nails that actually resembled claws on a grisly bear. She practice every day until she could use her nails as a deadly weapon,. Her advance towards Mallory of the Angels was stopped cold by the presence and quick action of Angel Gen. Noel. Moe was stunned at his quickness.

Because Moe used her finger and toe nails as weapons, Gen. Noel decided to keep his knife just in case it was needed. Circling each other, Noel could see the cruelty in Moe's eyes and prayed that this devil would not be allowed to approach and attack Mallory of the Angels. If she did, it would definitely be over for God's messenger.

Gen. Noel kept the fighting real close to each other. This basically eliminated Moe's use of toenails from the combat. Any time Moe would move back, Noel would move forward. It frustrated Moe so that she lost he patience and ran at full speed towards Noel. Noel, expecting this, tripped her as she ran passed him. The tripping caused Moe to fall and slide 30 feet on her face. You could almost taste the hate generated out of her thoughts. Slowly in getting up, Moe did not notice that Noel had placed himself behind her and threw mud and dirt into her eyes. Enraged and blind, Moe was swinging everwhere, constantly falling and injuring herself. Moe, exhausted, demoralized, and blinded with mud and dirt in her eyes, gave up and took Her own life rather than lose to one of God's Angels. Now only Lucifer was left. His choice - **Surrender of die**.

CHAPTER FIFTY-TWO - LUCIFER'S LAST STAND.

Lucifer's progress towards Mallory of the Angels was stopped abruptly by

Angel General Solrac, who by stepping in front of him, blocked Lucifer's vision. He could only to see Gen. Solrac's body in front of Him. These two great generals had seen each other in past battles. Each had a mutual respect for the other's capabilities. This fact, however, did not distract Gen. Solrac from proceeding with his mission. A mission that would capture Lucifer with minimal injuries and place Lucifer in a position to hear what Mallory of the Angels had to say.

In the fight, Lucifer at first, tried to box hand to hand with Gen. Solrac. After receiving several punches to his face, Lucifer changed tactics. This time he tried kick boxing. Again this did not help Lucifer. It only caused Lucifer to have painful shin splints. Lucifer began to fight Solrac with diffent styles of Karate and Kung Fu. He was able to score several kicks to the body, but most of them were sort of blocked, causing minor discomfort to Solrac. Lucifer, switching around to different styles of fighting, felt He was having an effect on Solrac. Lucifer could see Solrac giving ground, allowing for more attacks. Lucifer was thinking that with so many kicks and punches striking Solrac, pretty soon Lucifer would be getting the advantage over him. 30 minutes later, Lucifer felt that something was wrong. No matter how many blows He rained on Solrac, Solrac showed no wear and tear. In fact, Lucifer realized, He was the one who was getting tired. His arms and legs were heavy and sluggish. As the fight progressed, Lucifer noticed, that Solrac had not tried to injure or cause Him pain, even when the opportunity showed itself. Why was that?

Now Solrac began his attack of open handed slaps to Lucifer's face. Lucifer, being tired and having weary arms, could not stop all of the slaps aimed at his face. Lucifer felt like a little child being punished by his father. Still, the slaps continued to hit him in the face. Lucifer's face was beet red and showed the palm imprints of the slaps on his face. With his energy gone, his mouth and cheeks tender and sore, and his dignity gone, Lucifer pleaded for the beatings to stop. Gen. Solrac informed Lucifer that the beatings would stop if He, Lucifer, would pay attention to what Mallory of the Angels had to say. With fear of losing more of his dignity, Lucifer accepted Solrac's offer. God was notified. Proceed with God's plan,

CHAPTER FIFTY THREE - THE FIRES OF HELL ARE EXTINGUISHED.

Lucifer, while on his knees after His defeat by Angel Gen. Solrac, disgracefully noted that every level of His Hell was destroyed and occupied by **God's** Angel force. Lucifer expected no mercy and believed He would be decapitated in front on **God** and his Angels. Instead, Lucifer was escorted by Gen. Solrac, Gen. Samot, and Gen. Noel and seated before Mallory of the Angels.

Lucifer once believed that He was one of the most beautiful Angels, if not the most beautiful Angel in all of **God's** domain. Before Him stood Mallory of the Angels, the most loveliest, the most purest of Souls, the most brightest glow of Light and Love than He had ever seen or could have imagine.

Mallory of the Angels was an Angel loved by all Angels in Heaven. She had the purity of innocence, the Light of love and laughter, and a smile that would brighten the darkest Soul.

Mallory of the Angels was prepared as a child to be the Angel that would deliver **God's** message of Hope to Lucifer, once Hell was destroyed. For such a mission, the Angel chosen would have to be raised with tender love, with sincerity, honesty, and devotion to **God** and Jesus. Mallory of the Angels qualified in ever respect.

Lucifer and each Angel present in the place that was formally Hell, could see Mallory of the Angels very clearly as if She was looking and speaking directly to each of them.

Mallory of the Angels had a clear, soft, and gentle face. Her eyes were sparkling, with a blue-green color. Her hair was light brown that would wave with every gentle and soft breeze. She was radiant. Each room that Mallory walked in gave off a heavenly glow that would remain glowing hours after she departed. She had a heavenly body. Her wings were magnificent, spreading open to a full 70 feet. As Mallory was growing up, many thousands of Angels would place one of their feathers on her wings. The inner feathers were pure white, fluffy, and extremely soft to touch. The white feathers were trimmed with a rainbow of pastel colored feathers that only magnified the wing's brilliance. At will or when commanded by **God**, Her wings would glow so bright that no Soul could resist the promise of **God's** Love. Lucifer, on his knees, was wrapped in hope and in **God's** love. Now the message.

CHAPTER FIFTY-FOUR - GOD'S MESSAGE - TO ACCEPT OR NOT ACCEPT

Lucifer was very humbled. He had not yet seen **God** but all of God's goodness and God's strength was present. He faced Mallory of the Angels who had told him he had a choice to make. Standing behind and to the right of Him, was Angel Gen. Solrac. Gen. Solrac had his sword that was dipped in the mixture of Light, love, Jesus's blood, and Holy water blessed by God.

Gen, Solrac was to behead Lucifer at Mallory of the Angel's command.

Opening up her glowing wings to the full seventy feet, Mallory of the Angels magnified their brilliance and directed their light towards Lucifer.

Unable to blink, Lucifer was looking directly at **God's** immage. Unwinding the special scroll She held in Her hands, Mallory of the Angels began to read **God's** offer to Lucifer.

God, with His infinite goodness and love, has asked me, Mallory of the Angels, to offer you His Love, His Trust, and his Forgiveness, if you, Lucifer, would renounce all your evil ways, ask **God** for His forgiveness, and swear never again to take arms or advise other Angels to take arms against **God** or Heaven. If you, Lucifer, accept **God's** offer, you will be escorted to Heaven by Myself and My three Angel Generals. There in Heaven, **God** will bless you, cleanse your Soul, and allow you to once again, be an Angel in Heaven, Free to enjoy all the blessing, goodness, and happiness that dwell in the Heavens forever.

However, if you choose not to accept His offer, I, Mallory of the Angels, with **God's** blessing, will give the order for Gen. Solrac to decapitate you Causing you to disintegrate and you will cease to be in this or in any other world. You will no longer exist.

Lucifer asked if he accepted **God's** offer of forgiveness, will he remain a full status Archangel as he was before he broke off with **God.** He also wanted to know what happened to the Fallen Angels and the devils that requested **God's** forgiveness. Mallory of the Angels expressed to Lucifer that he would start off as an Archangel in training like the other 100 Fallen Angels now in Heaven. All other devils who requested forgiveness have been cleansed and given Basic Angel Status and enjoy the benefits and joy of Heaven. Lucifer was thinking to himself "Do I or don't I" accept **God's** offer"?

CHAPTER FIFTY-FIVE - LUCIFER MAKES HIS DECISION.

Lucifer remembered when He was a boy Angel, every Angel in Heaven was good to Him. He never needed for anything, as He was especially blessed by **God** to be one of Heaven's top Angels. He was given the best training, the uppermost of respect, and never for one second did he feel unloved. As He grew to full status of Archangel, He was given the highest trust and placed second in command of **God's** armies, seconed to

Michael the Archangel. At first he was happy and protected **God's** Kingdom against all enenmies. During a pitch battle with rogue devils, Lucifer was aked by one of these devils why He, Lucifer was not in command of all of **God's** Angels. This devil confessed to Him that the devils regarded him as the greatest warrior in all of heaven and Earth. After destroying that devil, Lucifer found himself jealous of Michael's position. With the power He commanded, Lucifer began to feel that not only was he a better warrior than Michael, but that he was just as powerful as **God** and at any time, He could replace **God**. He made his choice. He was able to convince ten thousands Archangels and fighting Angels to follow him and replace **God** and Michael the Archangel.

Consequently, in trying to replace **God**, He himself was defeated by Michael, His followers destroyed in a 10 year war. The surviving 100 Archangels were banished to hell with Lucifer. Now after so many centuries of living in Hell, (because Souls do not die unless killed by **God** or his forces), Lucifer, once again, is defeated in a battle with **God**. This time, however, a gracious **God** is giving Me a choice of Life or Death.

Lucifer was mixed up in His thinking. He had promised His devils that He would fight to the end. Now the end is here and He is still alive. Lucifer felt in his heart that He could not die, not without at least giving His life another chance.

Heaven had been very good to Him. Only His greed for power had changed Him and destroyed the goodness in Him. He remembered how much love He always received from the other Archangels and from **God** Himself. He realized that it was He, His fault, that his life turned bad and then to full evil. "I do not want to be a devil any more", he shouted at the top of his lungs. "I want to be back in God's love and I sincerely ask for **God's** forgiveness". Mallory of the Angels took Lucifer's hand and smiled.

God was immediately notified and the Heavens rejoiced.

"Mallory of the Angels"

Heaven was elated. The final devil has now repented and requested the forgiveness from **God**. **God** was extremely pleased. Befor Him stood Lucifer, kneeling and crying. Lucifer's head was bowed and His hands were outstretched towards **God**. "I want to be forgiven, my dearest **God**, for all the evil I committed against You and against Heaven". "I am truly sorry for what I have done to hurt You and the Heaven". Although I do not decerve your forgiveness, I humbly beg that you find it in your heart to forgive me and restore me back to one of your Angels in Heaven. "I will never again take arms against you or Heaven and I will not advise any other Angels to do so."

The Heavens were filled with love and forgiveness. Lucifer was forgiven by the Love of **God** and was restored to Archangel in training. With this new title, **God** also gave Lucifer a new name. His new new would be "**Archangel Gregorio**". No longer would He be called Lucifer. **God** declared "Hell is no longer. There is no evil on Earth as it is in Heaven".

Human life will continue with free choice so long as evil is not one of them.

Life on Earth will be as I created. i.e., peaceful and full of love for each other. Jealosy and segregation will no longer exist on Earth.

While the Heavens were celebrating the new Archangel Gregorio, **God** had requested the presence of Mallory of the Angels and her 3 general escorts. **God** was very proud of the work carried out by his Angel army, as well as bringing Gregorio back to Heaven and destroying Hell. But **God** was filled with much more pride and pure happiness as He had never felt before. The success of the entire mission was due to Mallory's pure heart and her true love and devotion to **God** and **Jesus**. Mallory of the Angels was a true warrior as well as a true healer. For her completion of the mission to end Hell and restore Gregorio back to Heaven, and for her full faith, **God** made Mallory the Angels "the **Archangel of Education**", Placing Mallory of the Angels in charge of all the training and education of all Archangels and all Angels in Heaven. To Gen. Solrac, Gen. Samot, and Gen. Noel, **God** had devided all of the Angel armies into three section with each of these Generals being placed in charge of one section. Michael the Archangel would remain to protect Heaven and the realm of **God**. **God's** last official order in the battle to defeat Hell was to appoint Gen. Dave G. To ensure that Lucifer's mansion and all levels of Hell were completely destroyed. **God's** dreams of peace and tranquility has come to pass. Heaven and Earth are one. What used to be Hell is now seven giant caves of flowing streams, beautiful flowers and trees kept beautiful with an eternal light that shines in from the heavens.

THE END

I was born in Ponce, Puerto Rico on July 10, 1944. My family moved to the United States when I was three years old. I grew up in a loving Christian family. I served in both the U.S. Navy and in the U.S. Army for a combined total of 25 years. During my military career, I obtained my Registered Nursing Degree. Currently I am a 100% Service Connected Disabled Veteran. I live at home in California with Marllory, my wife of 30 years. I have four wonderful children. I love traveling, writing poetry, reading western books by Louis L'Amour, cooking and enjoying what life has to offer me. I am truly proud to be an American and proud to live in America, the only country that protects the honor of God.

Printed in the United States
By Bookmasters